THE NEW GIRL

OAK BROOK ACADEMY, BOOK 1

JILLIAN ADAMS

D1519682

JILLIANADAMS.COM

ONE

Academic stimulation. That's what the brochure had described.

I ran my fingertips along the soft material of the blue Oak Brook Academy sweatshirt as I folded it. Just a piece of clothing and yet it made excitement bubble up within me as I added it to the stack inside the drawer. All different colors, all with the same emblem on the front—an oak tree overlooking a brook. Clever.

The only schools I'd ever been to were named after people— mostly presidents. This place was named after nature. I hoped that was a good sign.

I picked up the brochure that I'd tucked into my suitcase and looked it over again.

Yes, the stone buildings and cobblestone paths looked the same as pictured in the advertisement. Yes, there were plenty of lush gardens and even an Olympic-sized swimming pool that I'd glimpsed on the whirlwind tour I'd been given an hour ago by the house mother, Mrs. Reed.

But the smiling faces that stared up at me from the glossy paper? Those I hadn't seen at all.

I'd seen some odd looks and even a few glares, but mostly,

1

cold blank stares. Every student that I'd passed was dressed impeccably, as if they'd just wandered off the cover of a magazine and decided to explore what Oak Brook Academy had to offer.

The mix of boys and girls, all about my age, made me less enthusiastic about my chances of fitting in. Maybe there were some kids like me. Maybe they just weren't out walking on a beautiful spring afternoon.

Maybe Oak Brook Academy hid the nerds during tours.

"It's going to take some time for the other kids to warm up to you, Soph." My mother's voice jolted me out of my thoughts as her warm fingers swept through my long light brown hair. "Maybe if you smiled a little more?"

"Mom, kids don't warm up to me ever." I brushed her hand away and turned back to my suitcase. I didn't want her to see the disappointment on my face. I thought here it might be different. I thought maybe one good thing would come out of the tornado that was my mother's new husband. "I'll be fine." I shrugged.

"You don't have to stay here." She leaned closer to me, her dyed blonde hair hanging in clumps in front of her face as she whispered. "Just say the word and I'll take you back home with me. You can go to any school you want, it doesn't have to be this one." She frowned. "I'd rather have you closer to me."

"It's fine." I took a deep breath and forced a smile. "It's my first time ever in New York City. I'm really looking forward to exploring and I'm sure it will be great. This school is absolutely perfect. It has the best science program, and just about everyone that graduates from here goes on to an Ivy League school. It couldn't be better. Tell Dale I said thank you again."

"You don't have to keep thanking him, hon. He's your dad now." She winked at me. "It's his job to take care of you."

"Okay." I turned back to my suitcase.

At seventeen, I had no interest in having a dad. It had just been me and my mother for most of my life. What memories I had of my father were blurry and boring. Boots kicked off by the door. The smell of stale cigarettes. A bellowing voice asking for another beer.

I brushed the memories away. I'd been seven when he left, and even though I couldn't remember a single time that I'd liked having him around, it still sparked a bit of sadness inside me to think about the slam of the screen door.

I hadn't had the chance to get to know my mother's new husband well. They'd married a month after they had started dating. I met him for the second time at the wedding. He seemed nice enough. It didn't hurt that Dale happened to be wealthy and had very little interest in having me around. If that's what having him for a father meant, then I could play along for a few years.

"I think I'm all set here." I slid my hands into the pockets of my jeans and turned back to face my mother. "You can go."

"Are you sure?" She frowned as she scanned the room. "I feel like it could use more color. A lot more color."

"It's fine." I smiled as I looked at her bright pink blouse and her far too tight dark blue linen pants. My mother loved color. She always had. She'd once painted a wall in every shade she could find. We didn't get our security deposit back from that apartment.

"Listen, Sophie, I know this all seems wonderful to you, but don't let these kids get inside your head." She turned back to look at me. "Don't forget who you are." She looked straight into my eyes, as if we had some sort of secret.

If we did, I didn't know what it was.

I had no idea who I was.

"Sure. Thanks, Mom."

"Ugh, you've grown up just so fast!" She threw her arms around me and squeezed me tight.

I clenched my teeth but hugged her back.

"We hit the jackpot, sweetheart." She smiled as she pulled away. "This is it this time, I promise. We're going to be set for life."

"Just be careful, Mom."

My heart pounded as I saw that familiar gleam in her eye. How many times had I seen it before? Was Dale just another bump in the road? I hoped not. I hoped she would finally be happy, but I knew better. It wouldn't last.

But for as long as it did, I was going to get every drop of knowledge I could out of this school.

"Mom, you'd better get going. I'm sure Dale is waiting. I'll be fine."

"You're right." She sighed as she checked her phone. "Alright. Good luck, honey." She fluffed her fingers through my hair. "And please—baby, smile just a little? You're so pretty when you smile."

"Like this?" I smiled as wide as I could.

"Very funny." She rolled her eyes and walked out of the bedroom.

I heard the outer door of the dorm room close and breathed a sigh of relief.

Alone. Finally.

Seeing the dorm room for the first time had been a shock. It was more like an apartment than a dorm room. I had my own bedroom and so did my roommate, a girl I hadn't met yet. I had a brand new mattress on my bed—something that I'd never experienced before. A real dresser. Brand new clothes.

I looked at myself in the mirror that hung over the dresser and took a deep breath.

There I was, Sophie Blake—Queen Nobody—surrounded

by things far too expensive to ever belong to me. The same limp hair, the same too-pale skin and too-square figure.

But everything had changed, thanks to Oak Brook Academy. Thanks to my mother flirting with the right guy on the right plane at the right time. She'd always had a talent for attracting attention. Maybe that's why I found such comfort in being invisible.

Now, in this new place, I had to make a decision.

Was I going to continue to be part of the wallpaper or would I be willing to be seen?

The thought sent a shiver down my spine.

I looked back into my own eyes and leaned a little closer to the mirror. My mother's words echoed through my mind.

How could I remember who I was when I had no idea who that might be?

Here, in a place where education and intelligence were revered, the real me might just surface for the first time. Maybe, if I gave it a chance, things really would be different.

"Ick, why is that dirty ragged thing on my sofa?" The shrill voice that carried through the dorm room set my nerves on edge.

I braced myself as I walked through the bedroom door and into the living room.

There stood a raven-haired goddess, whom I guessed was my new roommate. She glared at the backpack I'd left on the sofa, then looked up at me.

No. Maybe things wouldn't be any different here at all.

TWO

"Sorry, that's mine." I felt myself shrink inside as her eyes probed every inch of my unremarkable existence. Instantly, I recalled third grade and the laughter of the girls who stood around me in a circle while I tried my hardest to hide the holes in my shirt. I'd known then that I would always be different.

"Why isn't it in the trash?" She poked at it with one perfectly manicured nail. "Don't you think it's time to put it out of its misery?"

I snatched up the frayed bag—I'd sewn the straps many times—and tossed it over my shoulder.

"Don't worry, I won't leave it out here again." The muscles in my legs burned with the urge to scurry back to my room and close the door. Hide, hide, hide, my mind chanted.

"Uh, that's not good enough." She grabbed me by the wrist and tugged me toward her room.

"What are you doing?" Flustered, I tried to wriggle free, but despite her slender frame, her grip didn't relent.

"Relax." She threw open the door to her bedroom and revealed a level of interior design that I would never expect in a dorm room.

Every piece of furniture was plush, while the fixtures and accent pieces were sharp and modern. Her queen-sized bed was piled with pillows that had words printed across them in languages I couldn't speak. One wall was covered with pictures —I assumed of places she'd visited. I wondered if there was anywhere in the world that she hadn't been.

She walked over to her closet door, still pulling me along behind her. She opened it. "Here." She tugged free a leather backpack, lined with what appeared to be silk and fur.

I recognized it from commercials I'd seen when school started at the beginning of the year. It was sold at one of the most exclusive stores in the country and the price tag that went with it was astronomical.

"Perfect." She turned back to me with a wide smile. "Do you like it?"

I stared at her. "It's very nice." I finally managed to get my hand free.

"Isn't it?" She grinned. "See the stitching?" She held it under her desk lamp. "It will never rip or wear. At least not for decades."

"Wow." I forced a smile as I tried to assess the point of it all.

"It's yours!" She shoved it toward me. "It's like a house-warming gift." She tipped her head to the side and smiled sweetly. "Welcome!"

"You want to give this to me?" I gingerly took it from her hand, a little concerned that the oil from my fingertips might blemish it forever.

"Yes, silly. There's no way you can walk these halls with that thing." She pointed to the bag on my shoulder. "Oak Brook is a lot of things, but accepting? Well, that's not one of them." She winked at me. "Go on, it's yours." She lowered her voice. "It's Gucci!"

"Oh, that's nice." I watched her expression in an attempt to figure out if she was serious or not. "Thanks for this, but I've used my backpack at every school I've ever been to and I think I'm going to stick with it." I offered her back the bag. "It's very nice of you, though."

"Oh, honey." She smiled as she looked at me. "It's not optional. You see, I'm already under the microscope here—due to my last roommate's poor decisions—and now—well, now I have you." She sat down on the edge of her bed and sighed. "I really can't afford anymore scandal in my life—after what happened to Jennifer—so I'm afraid you're just going to have to do as I say."

"What happened to Jennifer?" My heart skipped a beat as I wondered if she had been chewed up and spit out by my new roommate.

"You didn't hear this from me, but..." She patted her stomach and widened her eyes. "She had to take care of some *family issues*."

"She was pregnant?" I blurted the words out.

"Shh!" She frowned. "It's not something we talk about."

I stared at her. I'd known of a few girls in my previous schools who'd gotten pregnant. It wasn't ever a good thing, but they didn't vanish either. It was just something that happened.

"Was she kicked out?" My chest tightened at the thought. I couldn't imagine losing the opportunity to attend a school like this.

"The details are pretty murky. Let's just say that an arrangement was made and now you're here." She smiled at me, then thrust her hand out. "I'm Mabel, by the way." She rolled her eyes. "My parents thought an old-fashioned name would be sweet. People call me Maby."

"Like maybe? As in perhaps?" I shook her hand as I raised an eyebrow. "I'm Sophie."

"Yes, just like maybe." She laughed and shook her head.

"Nicknames stick around here. It won't be long before you're Fifi."

"Never." I took a step back.

"Do you think I wanted to be Maby?" She smirked. "Alright, I'll take you to the meet-up tonight, but you can't wear that. Let's see what else you have." She brushed past me into my room.

As I trailed after her I wondered what the meet-up was and why she'd agreed to take me to it when I hadn't asked. My heart pumped faster as I tried to keep up with Maby's words.

"During the week we have uniforms we have to wear. I started a protest about it, but so far Principal Carter hasn't budged." She sifted through the clothes in my closet. "Are these yours?" She looked over at me, her eyes wide.

"Yes." I rubbed my hand along my arm as I noticed her adorable tiny nose crinkle in what could only be described as disgust.

"Maybe I can work with this." She pulled a blouse out of the closet and tossed it on the bed.

"Actually, I'd rather just stay in tonight. I want to go over some of the course work. I may be a little behind." I frowned. "I haven't exactly had this kind of education before."

"Oh, honey, no one has had this kind of education before." She turned to look at me, then sighed. "Listen, I get that you've got this sweet shy girl thing going on, but that's not going to fly here, Fi. You're swimming with sharks now and if they sense a drop of blood in the water, they'll tear you to tiny shreds." She clapped her hands together.

"It's Sophie." I cleared my throat. "It's alright, I'm sure it can't be worse than what I'm already used to."

"It can be and it is." She stepped right in front of me and looked into my eyes. "I'm going to do everything I can to protect you, Sophie, but you have to be willing to work with me. Otherwise, you won't last the week."

"The academic opportunities, the chance that I could go to an excellent college—that's what brought me to Oak Brook. I'm here to learn, that's all." I crossed my arms.

Although Maby kept insisting that she was my friend, I sensed that things could go either way. Was that quiver in her voice just her being extra dramatic or was there something behind it?

"You will." Her voice softened as she glanced toward the large window beside my bed. "There's no question about that." She looked back at me, her eyes narrowed. "If you think you can do this on your own, good luck. I'm not going to force you to keep your head above water. But if you decide that it might actually be better to have a friend, just let me know. You think you know what school is like, but this isn't school, Fi. This is an entirely different world."

My heart fluttered as I sensed the certainty in her voice. I'd read stories about boarding schools—dramatic creations of fiction where the kids ran the school and everyone behaved in ways that would make the most manipulative criminal blush.

But those were just stories. Not real life. Right?

I picked up the blouse from the bed.

"What's the meet-up?" I met her eyes.

"Good girl." Maby smiled. "Don't worry, you're going to love it. Get changed. And please, put your hair up or something." She tossed the backpack on my bed as she shook her head and walked out of my room.

I heard the door close and took a deep breath. Perhaps Maby was right about keeping my head above water. I did already feel like I was drowning.

THREE

I changed into the blouse that Mabel had selected for me. It was one of my least favorite shirts because the neck hung low and the material had a gauzy feel to it. But I still put it on. I pulled my hair back into a ponytail and hoped that it was what she'd meant by "put it up." I made sure it wasn't too high or bouncy.

When I stepped out of my bedroom, I found her in the living room waiting for me.

"Much better." She nodded, though there wasn't much enthusiasm in her voice. "At least it will do for now. I'm sure the boys will be eager to check you out no matter what you're wearing. They're always looking for someone new." She walked toward the door. "Let's go! Everyone is probably already there."

"Everyone?"

I fell into step behind her as I wondered about these eager boys she'd mentioned. Had she told me to change to please them? The thought set me off balance. I'd never attempted to look a certain way for a boy before and often found it ridiculous when other girls did.

"Where are we going exactly?"

"You'll see." She led me down the nearby stairs.

Our dorm room was on the third floor, which I loved, as it gave me a great view of the sprawling green grounds. I had no idea how they managed to fit so much nature onto a property in the middle of the city, but so far, the school's location on the Upper East Side was nothing like what I pictured Manhattan to be.

"Mabel, aren't we supposed to be going to the cafeteria for dinner?" I glanced at my watch. "On my schedule it says—"

"Dinner is never on time. We show up about an hour after the schedule says, otherwise you'll be sitting there waiting forever. Usually we meet up before dinner, after dinner, and after lunch." She pushed open the tall door that guarded the entrance of the girls' dormitory.

"Who's *we*? All of the students?" I couldn't resist asking questions. Everything was so new and I wanted to have a handle on exactly what I was walking into.

"No, not all of them." Mabel walked right past the boys' dormitory across the courtyard from ours and continued around behind the building. She headed straight for the grassy area behind the dorms.

I knew already, from reading the rules that Mrs. Reed had given me, that leaving the main grounds of the campus was not allowed unless permission had been given.

"Uh—Mabel, are you sure we should be going this way?"

"It's Maby, remember, Fi?" She smirked over her shoulder at me. "You're either with us or you're not." She met my eyes. "Trust me, you'd much rather be with us."

"I don't want to get into trouble on my first day." Or ever, I thought to myself.

"Trust me, Fi." She grabbed my hand and smiled. "I told you I'd protect you."

Something about the way she said it made me even more uneasy. I wondered if I was a person to her or just an object that now belonged to her. The old me would have turned around and walked right back into the dormitory, but the new me—this strange Sophie that liked the mystery of a secret place—was too curious to pull away.

As we neared the edge of the grounds, though, my curiosity began to be overcome by my fear of breaking rules.

"No, this is too far, I'm going back."

"Seriously?" She turned to face me. "If you're going to make it past dinner, you need to loosen up a bit."

"I don't want to loosen up. I just want to do whatever I need to do to stay here." I took a step back. "I think you're trying to be nice to me, and I appreciate that, but this just isn't me."

"You don't even know what this is yet." She laughed, then crossed her arms. "Alright, I'll tell you what. You come with me now, and if you don't like what you see, then I'll never ask you to come with me again."

Don't do it. It's that simple, Sophie, just don't do it. Don't follow this girl down some weird rabbit hole and lose everything you've dreamed of in just one day.

She held her hand out to me.

I took it. I took it and felt every muscle in my body tighten.

She grinned, then tugged me through some tall bushes.

As soon as we stepped through the bushes, we stepped onto pavement. It startled me at first. One second I was on a lush green lawn, the next I was in an alley and off the school grounds.

It was too late to turn back. I'd already broken a rule.

"Where are we?" I had a hard time taking a breath.

"Relax, we're just near the supply buildings." She tugged me around behind one of the buildings, through another alley, and into an empty parking lot surrounded by more buildings.

I glanced back over my shoulder, unsure if I could find my way back.

"These are just used for storage." Maby looked up at the tall buildings. "Amazing how much stuff they can shove in them. It's part of an old section of the campus. Instead of updating the buildings, they just built new ones." She tipped her head toward the one to her right. "This one belongs to us."

"Belongs to you? How?" I stumbled forward as she pulled me in the direction of the building.

When she threw the door open, I was greeted by glowing lights and a strange assortment of fabrics and random decorative items strewn in different parts of the large space. Lampshades hung from Christmas lights, a bed was piled up with pillows to resemble a sofa, and office chairs of every size and color littered the interior.

"Is this the new girl? Are you sure about this?" A tall girl stepped out from behind one of the curtains. "What if she tells?"

"She's not going to tell." Maby rolled her eyes. "Candy, you're so paranoid."

"I'm not paranoid. But look at her." She crossed her arms as she met my eyes. "She's not exactly one of us."

"Not yet." Another girl stepped out from behind the curtain. "But she has potential." She thrust her hand out in my direction. "I'm Apple."

"Sophie." I shook her hand, then smiled. "Or, I guess, Fi. Just like you're Candace, right?" I looked at Candy. "And I'm not sure what Apple is a nickname for..." I looked back at the girl in front of me.

Candy and Maby laughed. Apple winced.

"It's not a nickname." She sighed. "It's my real name."

"We were calling her Seed and then Seedy, but it just got a little out of hand." Maby shrugged. "So we just stick with Apple."

"It's great." Apple rolled her eyes.

"I think it's pretty." I smiled.

"Oh, she's too sweet." Apple laughed and flounced her dark hair back over her shoulders. "Wait until Wes gets a taste of her."

"We're going to keep her away from Wes!" Maby narrowed her eyes.

"We'd be better off keeping her away from Chuckles." Candy pursed her lips. "I can't believe he's still here."

"Never mind about that." Maby draped her arm around my shoulder. "We don't want to scare her off."

Wes and Chuckles already sounded pretty scary. I wasn't sure what to think as Maby led me further into the room.

"Hurry up!" a voice shouted from outside the door. A male voice.

My heart jumped into my throat. The pitch of the voice made me think it was a student, but what if it wasn't?

The door burst open and a boy with dark hair and dark eyes to match stumbled inside with a laugh. He clutched a football in his grasp as if he'd just caught it.

"Hello, ladies." He straightened up and flashed a smile at them.

"No balls inside! Remember?" Candy huffed and put her hands on her hips. Her short red hair bounced around her cheeks as she shook her head. "You're not going to wreck the place."

FOUR

"No balls inside?" He smirked as he looked into Candy's eyes. "Don't you think that rule could be a problem?"

"Give me that." Another boy stepped inside after the first. He was taller, with chestnut-brown hair that brushed the curves of his ears. He looked at the first boy with a sharp glare and snatched the football from his hands. "If you're going to bring a ball inside, you have to do it properly." He pulled his arm back and aimed the ball at Candy. "Go long!"

"Wes, don't you dare!" Candy gasped and raised her hands to cover her face.

The thought of the football striking Candy in the face snapped my body into action. Before I had time to think about what I was doing, I snatched the football from Wes's hands and pinned it close against my chest.

"Hey!" Wes turned to look at me in the same moment that I backed up into an old coat rack that had been transformed into a place to hang artwork. The coat rack wobbled and I shuddered as Wes's bright green eyes collided with mine. "I was just kidding around." He frowned as he studied me.

"My hero!" Candy pretended to swoon as she smiled at me.

"See, Wes, you'd better not mess with me, because Fifi has my back. Don't you, Fi?"

I resisted the urge to correct her. What would be the point? Maby had labeled me Fifi and now I was Fifi.

"Fifi, huh?" Wes's lips spread into a smile. "The new girl."

"It's Sophie." It came out of my mouth a whisper as Wes stared at me.

"Isn't she adorable?" Maby gave my ponytail a light tug.

"Are you going to give me my ball back?" He held out his hand for the football.

Something about the way he looked at me made me uneasy. It fell somewhere between curiosity and annoyance.

"Here." I handed the ball over to Candy, then I edged around the coat rack and further into the hideout of my classmates.

I had no idea whether these kids were going to be my friends or not, but I was certain that I wasn't interested in getting to know Wes better. Already he had shown me that he liked to cause trouble. I couldn't deny that he was attractive—in a deodorant commercial kind of way—but that didn't change the fact that he didn't seem terribly intelligent.

"Ouch." He quirked an eyebrow, then looked over at his friend. "It looks like we'll have to watch out for this one, huh, Mick?"

"It's my ball!" Mick frowned and snatched it out of Candy's hands. "I wasn't going to do anything with it."

"I'm sure you weren't." Maby purred and walked over to him. "Don't get all ruffled, Mick. We're all here to have some fun, right?"

"Sure." He flopped down onto the bed-turned-sofa and sighed. "If I have to get up before sunrise one more time, I swear I'm going to take Coach Baker out."

"You and what army?" Apple laughed as she plopped down

beside him. "Coach Baker could take both of you out with a few swings of those amazing biceps."

"They're not that amazing." Mick winced. "Have you seen mine lately?" He rolled the sleeve of his shirt up and revealed a muscular arm.

"Take it easy, Mick, you don't want to give Fifi here the wrong impression about us." Wes pulled a bottle of soda from a cooler beside the coat rack and offered it to me.

"No thanks." I forced a smile to be polite.

"You might want to take it, the cafeteria only serves cucumber water and coconut milk. Thanks to Apple's parents." He shot a playful glare in Apple's direction.

"I'm sorry!" She groaned and flopped back against the cushions. "I can't help it if they believe in clean eating."

"Take it." Maby nodded. "Trust me."

"Thanks." I took the bottle but did my best to avoid looking at Wes. When my fingers brushed against his, my heart began to pound.

Ridiculous. I closed my eyes for a moment.

"You okay?" Wes took a step closer to me. "You know, I wasn't going to throw the ball at her."

"I don't know that, no." I took another step back and collided with the solid wall, hidden behind a wispy curtain.

"I wouldn't hurt her." He frowned.

"He's right." Candy grabbed a soda from the cooler as well. "He was just playing around."

I nodded. I had nothing more to say about it. To me, threatening to cause harm was always a serious thing.

"I'm a pussycat. Really." He leaned against the wall beside me. "You'll see."

"That's alright, I'll just take your word for it." I shifted further away from him. So far I didn't see anything great about hanging out with Maby's friends.

"Fifi, don't be so harsh." Maby blew me a kiss. "Don't mind her, Wes, she's from the real world."

"The real world?" Mick sat up. "Are you serious?" He looked over at me.

Confused, I shrugged and wished I could disappear.

"Public school," Maby whispered as if it was some kind of curse. "She's seen it all!"

"Is that true?" Candy gasped as her eyes widened. "Have you seen a murder? Has someone tried to murder you? Oh! Have you murdered someone?" She snapped her fingers. "I'll bet she has! That's why she's so quiet."

"Don't be stupid!" Apple frowned. "They wouldn't let a murderer into Oak Brook." She glanced over at Maby. "Would they?"

"Who knows?" Maby smirked. "They let Wes in, didn't they?"

"I'm not a murderer." I rolled my eyes. "I haven't seen any murders and I haven't almost been murdered. I'd really just like to go back to my dorm room now." I started to walk back toward the door, but Maby caught my wrist.

"Don't be so cranky. We were just teasing." She pulled me down onto the bed beside her. "We come here to relax. All that stress and tension—that has to stay outside the fort."

"Aren't you all a little old for playing pretend?" I ran my gaze along each of their faces. I guessed that Apple and Mick might be sixteen, but I was pretty sure the rest were at least seventeen. I wrenched my hand free and stood up from the bed. "Look, I'm not interested in whatever this is supposed to be."

"It's not pretend." Wes stepped in front of the door before I could reach it. His playful smile had faded and the stern gaze he settled on me made his features appear sharper. "It's our place."

"Move, I want to go." I shivered as I realized that there was no way for me to make him move.

"Not yet." Candy stood up and walked over to me.

"You can't keep me hostage here!" I spun around to face her.

"Wow, calm down, Fi." Maby glared at me. "You should be grateful we included you. We didn't have to."

"Well, I'm not grateful. I just want to leave." I turned back to Wes again. "If you don't get out of my way, I will make you."

"Is that so?" Wes grinned as he took a step toward me.

"Enough!" Apple stepped between us. "Listen, we need to all calm down."

"How can I calm down when she's about to go tell Mrs. Reed about all this?" Candy shook her head. "We can't let her do that."

"I'm not telling anyone." I held up my hands. "What you do out here is your business. I just want out."

"Fi, you haven't even given us a chance." Maby crossed her arms. "I thought you were supposed to be smart?"

I took a step toward Wes as my eyes began to burn with tears. I was prepared to throw an elbow or a kick if I had to.

Wes looked into my eyes, then stepped aside. "Let her go. She doesn't belong here anyway."

FIVE

It wasn't easy to find my way back to the dormitory, but once I did, I realized that it wasn't far enough for me to get away. Soon Maby would return and I'd be faced with the embarrassment of her judgment. It made my skin crawl to think of Wes looking at me the way that he had.

She doesn't belong here anyway.

His words echoed through my mind.

He wasn't wrong. I slumped down on my bed and closed my eyes. I didn't belong here. I was smart enough—I hoped—but that didn't mean I could ever fit in. It seemed hopeless that I would ever fit in anywhere. I'd been singled out—and at times even attacked—at every school I'd ever been to. I tried to be kind, I tried to be mean, I once even slugged a boy that wouldn't stop flicking the back of my head. But I'd never managed to be the right person in the right moment to make any real friends.

"Maybe I am the problem." I kicked my shoes off and stretched out on the bed. At least the mattress felt amazing. How long would I get to sleep in this bed before something happened that burst the bubble my stepfather's wealth had wrapped around me?

A soft chime played repeatedly. As I thought back to the tour Mrs. Reed had given me, I recalled her indication of the speakers on the walls in the hallways. They were used to notify students when it was time to change classes, when it was time for lunch, and when it was time for dinner.

I looked at my watch and frowned. Right. Dinner. I'd have to walk into that huge cafeteria with no one to sit with. Not to mention the fact that Maby and her friends would likely be angry at me.

But if I didn't go, I would already be presenting a poor image of myself to Mrs. Reed and the other adults in charge of my future here.

"Fine." I grunted as I stood up from the bed. "It's not like I haven't dealt with this before."

I changed out of the blouse that Maby had picked out for me and into a plain white t-shirt.

I headed out of the dorm room. My footsteps echoed through the long halls. The sound bounced off the many paintings and over golden vases and bouquets of flowers, to settle in my ears.

Alone, alone—the thuds seemed to chant.

Down the stairs, out through the front door to the building that was nestled in between the boys' and girls' dormitories. I could have taken the long way through the halls that held the classrooms, but I'd decided it was best to get it over with.

When I pulled the door open and stepped into the entrance of the common building, there was no one to greet me. But snippets of laughter, shouts, and conversation drifted toward me from the hallway to the right.

To my left was a large living room and beyond that I knew there was a game room, complete with pool table and arcade machines. It was apparent that Oak Brook Academy spared no expense to keep its students happy.

I tugged at the collar of my shirt and took a deep breath. Then I pushed the door to the cafeteria open and prepared myself for the usual torture. There were rows of tables—many of which were occupied. And everyone seemed to be avoiding looking in my direction as I scouted for a place out of the way to sit.

Things seemed to be a little different at Oak Brook Academy, however. For one, the tables were round and well-spaced. There was an open buffet filled with food, much of which I'd never even tasted before. Everything from seafood to steak looked fresh, and the smells that filled the cafeteria danced through my senses.

My stomach growled. Was it as loud as it seemed? I dared to look up to see if anyone had noticed.

"Fi!" Maby stood up and waved to me from her table. Apple, Candy, and Mick were there. So was Wes.

My heart pounded. It was a trick, wasn't it?

I turned my attention to the buffet table and began to place food onto my plate. As I neared the end, I sensed the presence of another person. I held my breath, afraid to know who it was.

"Don't eat that." A hand reached between my line of sight and my plate, then snatched a lobster claw off it.

"Huh?" I looked up and immediately regretted it. Those green eyes locked to mine and every single muscle in my body tensed at the same time.

"Trust me." Wes tossed it into the garbage can located not far from the buffet. "They're always overcooked."

I would have told him that I didn't care if it was overcooked —I'd never had lobster on my plate before—but I couldn't get my lips to move.

He quirked an eyebrow, then leaned closer to me. "You okay?"

"Fine." I forced the word out, then stepped to the side in an attempt to avoid him.

"This way." He placed his hand on my back and steered me toward Maby's table.

I noticed that all eyes in the room had settled on me—or more specifically, on me and Wes. The other students whispered to one another as they huddled around their tables. If I pulled away from him, what would they think then?

I frowned as I realized that I'd gotten myself tangled up with the popular crowd.

"That's alright, I'd rather sit by myself." I spotted an empty table and started to change direction.

"Sophie." He murmured my name as his fingertips swept along my back. "Don't make it hard on yourself. Sit with us and no one will touch you. Sit by yourself..." He tipped his head toward the empty table. "And you're going to become a target." He leaned his lips near my ear and whispered. "I know you're smarter than that."

His voice sent a shiver down my spine. Hatred or something even more primal threatened to burst out of me. Was I more angry that Wes seemed to be having an effect on me or that he was probably right?

I pulled away from him to sit in one of the empty chairs at Maby's table.

"You've made some good choices." Maby grinned as she eyed my plate. Then she stole a piece of roasted asparagus. "My favorite." She took a bite.

I braced myself. Surely, this was some kind of prank.

"Look, I won't tell anyone, alright?" I looked at each of them at the table. "You don't have to worry about me."

"Worry?" Candy shook her head. "We're not worried. If you try to say a word about our fort, we'll just spread some nasty rumor about you." She wiggled her eyebrows. "Maybe about you and Wes?"

"Ugh—please, no." I winced.

"You should be so lucky." Wes rolled his eyes.

"Easy, Wes." Maby shot a glare in his direction, then looked back at me. "Relax, Fi, we're just being friendly. What has happened to you to make you so paranoid?"

A list of the dreadful things that had been done to me in the past by bullies and people who'd claimed to be my friends began to fill my mind. But as I met Maby's eyes, I couldn't bring myself to share the details.

"I'm sorry, I'm just not used to any of this."

"I understand." Maby smiled at me, then took my hand. "But here's the deal. We're roommates. We have to make this work. I will not give up my room. I have it decorated just the way I want it. If you and I can't get along, then I will be the one they move. I've already lost one roommate this year, I don't want to lose another."

"Speaking of..." Wes leaned back in his chair as a boy approached the table.

I looked up at him and noticed the way his eyes skated from Maby to Wes, then to the others.

"Can I still sit here?" He frowned.

"I don't know, Chuckles—can Jennifer?" Maby locked her eyes to his.

SIX

"Maby." Mick sighed. "Let it go. It's not like it didn't take both of them to make it happen."

"And?" Maby frowned. "That doesn't mean he gets to sit here."

"It's fine, I get it." Chuckles backed away from the table.

"Harsh, Maby." Apple shook her head. "He's our friend."

"So was—is—Jennifer." Maby picked up her glass and took a sip.

I watched as Maby's fingers wrapped tighter around the glass. Whatever issue she had with Chuckles, it still appeared to be bothering her.

"So Jennifer had to leave, but nothing happened to him?" I met her eyes as she looked at me.

"We're not supposed to talk about it." Apple picked at her plate of food.

"Since when do we follow the rules?" Wes picked up a roll and took a bite.

"She wasn't forced to leave." Candy crossed her arms. "She just wasn't exactly welcome to stay."

"Are you kidding?" Maby shook her head. "Principal Carter never would have let her stay."

"She wanted to go." Mick's voice softened.

"They were best friends," Apple whispered to me.

I stared at Maby. Perhaps there was more to her than I'd first assumed. She wasn't just a beautiful, spoiled, rich girl. She'd lost her best friend and was still reeling from it. I imagined that would be painful.

"I'm sorry, Maby."

"Sorry for what?" She raised an eyebrow as she turned her attention back to me. "Sorry for that pathetic shirt or sorry for throwing a tantrum earlier?"

Her sharp tone surprised me. I sank back against my chair as I thought about how alone I'd felt not long before.

"Sorry for sitting here." I snapped in return and picked up my tray.

As I walked over to the empty table, I heard a ripple of chatter all around me. I didn't care. Let them all turn against me. *That* I was used to. *That* I could handle. But I wasn't going to be toyed with.

As I sat down and finished my dinner, I expected to feel regret. Instead, I felt a little bit of power. I'd come to this school for a reason and it wasn't to make friends with people like Maby and Wes.

I waited until a lot of the other students had left the cafeteria, then I carried my tray back to the kitchen. The food had been delicious—a far cry from anything I'd ever eaten in a high school cafeteria before. That was one bright spot in my day.

I thought about Jennifer and the way her life must have changed. That was one thing I didn't have to worry about. I'd never even kissed a boy before, unless my neighbor down the street counted.

We were only ten. I didn't think it counted.

When I stepped out of the cafeteria into the hall that led to the common rooms, I heard voices and laughter. I didn't belong in the middle of that.

I headed for the hall that led past the classrooms and into the dormitories. I was almost to the door when I heard a familiar voice call out to me.

"Sophie, this is free recreation time." Mrs. Reed smiled as she caught up with me at the door. "You're welcome to use the living room or the game room. There are a few kids outside on the tennis court if you'd like to try that."

"No, thanks, I'm just going to go back to my room." I forced a smile, then turned toward the door.

"I know first days can be hard." Her warm fingers landed on my shoulder in a subtle pat. "I noticed you sitting alone at dinner."

"I like a little space." I frowned as I looked back at her. I realized I wasn't getting out of this conversation easily.

"A little space is fine, but part of the experience here at Oak Brook Academy is developing friendships that will last a lifetime." She searched my eyes. "Are you homesick?"

"Homesick." I smiled at the thought. I'd never really had a home to speak of. My mother and I moved around so much. "No, I'm not homesick. It's just been such a busy day. I'm a little worn out, I guess."

"Okay, I understand that. But if you ever need to talk, just know that I'm here." She smiled. "My door is always open."

"Thanks." I nodded to her, then pushed through the door that led to the next building. All I really wanted to do was forget the entire day. I wanted to forget about Maby and Jennifer and especially Wes. I wanted to focus only on the luxury I was surrounded by and how much better my future would be when I graduated from Oak Brook Academy.

If I could just make it that long.

I stepped into my empty dorm room and breathed a sigh of relief.

I hurried into my bedroom, closed the door, and locked it. If Maby didn't want to be my friend, I was fine with that, but I didn't want her bursting into my room unannounced. I didn't plan to give her any opportunity to harass me.

I curled up in my bed and closed my eyes.

I must have been more exhausted than I realized, because when I opened my eyes, the clock on my bedside table showed that it was six in the morning.

I'd slept all night.

I sat up and stretched my arms above my head. I hadn't even changed into pajamas. I smacked my lips as I realized that I hadn't brushed my teeth either.

I turned on the shower in my bathroom to let the water get warm and brushed my teeth while I waited. Maybe I could stay in my room the whole day today, but tomorrow I had classes that I had to show up for. That meant seeing other people.

I knew I would have to bite the bullet and try to get to know some other students. Just because Maby and her friends had turned out to be people I wanted to avoid, that didn't mean there weren't still some options out there. I just had to make an effort.

Social interaction had never been a skill of mine. In fact, I was more talented at avoiding it. But if I was going to survive Oak Brook, I needed to at least try to find a few allies.

I stepped out into a dark living room and crept toward the door. Before I could get far, I heard a subtle snore. My heart lurched at the sound.

I took a sharp breath as I spun around to find Maby asleep on the sofa. Her blanket hung half off her and she shivered as she turned into the cushions.

My mind flashed back to the times I'd found my mother in a similar position.

Before I knew it, my hands had curled around the edge of the blanket and I tugged it back up over Maby's shoulders. As I pulled my hand away, her eyes fluttered open and she looked straight into mine.

"Fi."

"I'm sorry." I took a step back. "You looked cold." I started toward the door.

"Wait, please." Maby sat up on the sofa.

"I didn't mean to wake you." I stopped at the door and looked back at her.

"It's okay." She patted the space beside her. "Will you sit for a minute?"

Maybe it was the dim lighting or the fact that the sun wasn't quite up yet, but Maby looked different to me. She didn't look quite as perfect. Were her eyes puffy?

Against my better judgment, I sat down beside her. "Are you okay?"

"You ask me that after the way I treated you?" She smiled. "That's why I like you, Fi."

"You do?" I raised an eyebrow.

"I do. I'm sorry about yesterday." She rested her head against the back of the sofa and stared up at the ceiling. "I miss Jennifer. I didn't think it would bother me this much."

It struck me that maybe we were both lonely, both faced with a similar problem.

"If you ever want to talk, I'm here." I bit into my bottom lip. It felt awkward to make the offer to someone I barely knew, but in that moment, I felt as if I might be all that Maby had.

"Thanks, Fi." She smiled.

SEVEN

For the rest of Sunday, Maby showed me around campus. She showed me the things that weren't on the tour.

There was a fountain where everyone tried to get chewed-up wads of gum to stick to the head of the statue in the middle. There was the corner of one of the buildings where names of students who were kicked out were etched into infamy.

I noticed that Jennifer's name was there.

Maby didn't say a word about that.

There were three libraries, but one—the smallest—was considered a hideaway as it was so infrequently used.

At lunch she introduced me to the hallway filled with pictures and souvenirs from many school trips. By the time we'd all gathered at our table, I felt more comfortable with Oak Brook Academy and with Maby. Then Wes sat down beside me.

"Back for more, huh?" He leaned toward me. "You just don't learn, do you?"

"She's with me." Maby looked straight at Wes. "Be nice."

"I'm always nice." He grinned. "Tell her, Candy." He winked at Candy.

"Wes won't hurt her." Candy rolled her eyes. "He's harmless."

"I find that hard to believe." I eyed him with a touch of annoyance. The way he always seemed to smile no matter what he said, his laid-back attitude, and his insistence on looking at me, all added up to my not wanting to be anywhere near him.

"Do you?" He rested his head on his hand and looked straight at me. "Maybe you just need to get to know me better."

"Pass." I picked up my fork and dug into my lasagna.

"She's quick." Mick laughed. "We might have a genius on our hands."

"That hurts, Fi." Wes pressed his hand against his chest and leaned back in his chair. "It really does."

I noticed the glint of amusement in his eyes as he looked at me. Why did they have to be so green? Why did his hair drape across his forehead in just the right way? Why was my heart beating faster the longer he looked at me?

"Leave her alone." Apple tossed a piece of her roll at Wes. "You've done enough damage at this table. Go fishing somewhere else."

"Alright, I will." Wes stood up and walked over to a nearby table where mostly female students sat. He leaned his hands on the edge of their table, said something, and they all began to giggle.

"Oh my." Maby rolled her eyes and laughed. "You've set him loose now, Apple. We're going to be mopping up broken hearts in no time."

"Please, everyone knows who Wes is. If they want to take the risk of getting involved with him, it's their own fault."

Those words stuck with me for the rest of the day. It seemed as if everywhere I went, Wes was there. He had his arm around one girl in the game room while we all played pool. He ran his fingers through the hair of another girl as we sat in the courtyard after dinner. When Maby and I headed back to our dorm room, I caught sight of him with yet another girl as he steered her toward the small library, his arm tight around her waist.

"Don't let him bother you." Maby smiled when she caught me looking in his direction. "He's got more ego than bite. He just likes to know he can wrap them around his finger. In the three years we've both attended this school, I've never seen him with a girlfriend for more than a week or two."

"And that doesn't bother you?" I followed her up the stairs toward our room.

"No, it doesn't, and once you get to know him, it probably won't bother you either. Wes acts like he's untouchable, but that's all a show."

Curiosity bubbled up within me, but I resisted the urge to ask more questions. I didn't want to get to know Wes better. In fact, I hoped that I would be able to avoid him completely.

When my alarm went off the next morning, I woke up with a jolt.

Monday morning. First day of classes.

I dressed quickly and made sure I had everything I needed in my book bag. It really did smell better than my old one.

I met Maby for some breakfast in our small kitchen and then we walked off in different directions to our classes.

When I opened the door to the classroom, I smiled.

There it was. The smell of freshly polished floors, notebook paper, and sharpened pencils. Despite the difficulties I'd faced in school, those smells still inspired a sense of excitement in me. Once I had my nose buried in a book, none of my worries would matter anymore. No matter what, Oak Brook Academy offered me the opportunity to have a real education and that thrilled me —until I spotted the boy sitting in the back of the room beside the only empty desk.

"Wes." His name popped out of my mouth before I could stop it.

"Fi." He grinned as he met my eyes. "I saved a seat for you." He pointed to the empty desk.

From the laughter in his voice, I sensed that he enjoyed making me as uncomfortable as possible.

I looked helplessly at the teacher.

"That desk will have to do for now. All the other seats have already been assigned for the year." She handed me a tablet. "I'm Mrs. Davis. Wes can tell you what page we're on. Let's all get started on the next section." She turned her attention back to the rest of the class.

I stared down at the tablet. So much for burying my nose in a book.

I walked back toward the empty desk. I found interesting things to look at on the walls, on the floor, and out through the window that faced the courtyard. I did everything I could to avoid Wes's eyes. As I sat down in my chair, I could sense the weight of his gaze still on me. Did he expect me to thank him?

"Chapter eight," he muttered.

"What?" I shot a brief look in his direction.

"I thought you were smart?" He pushed a frustrated breath through his teeth. "We're on chapter eight."

"Oh, right." I blinked, then looked down at the tablet on my desk. I navigated to the right chapter and began to read over the content.

Briefly, I lost myself in the poetry that scrolled across the page. I would have liked to run my fingers over the thin paper of a real book, but the words themselves made up for the weight and coldness of the tablet in my hand. I drifted through the content and for a short time I forgot all about Wes sitting only a few feet from me.

As the class came to an end and the teacher began to speak about an assignment, I looked up at her.

"Each of you will be paired up to create a poem similar to what we have read today. Poetry is a very personal endeavor, but I find that working with a partner can inspire students to look deeper and be more honest." She began to list off the names of the paired-up students. "And Wesley, you and Sophie will work together on this one. Please make sure that you catch her up on the way presentations are given." Mrs. Davis pushed her glasses up along her nose. "And don't forget that this assignment counts for a large amount of your final grade." She held up one hand as the students groaned. "I don't give tests, I told you this from the beginning. I want to see creativity. I want to see honesty. In this particular assignment, I want to be able to feel your emotions." She walked along the first aisle of desks. "Dig deep. Explore feelings that you might have bottled up over the years. Do whatever it takes to get something real down on paper for me." She paused beside my desk and smiled. "If you have any questions you can always send me an e-mail, Sophie. I hope you're enjoying your first day so far."

"It's great. Thanks." I spoke through gritted teeth.

If I said what I really wanted to say, I'd be the next name added to that wall outside.

EIGHT

Why of all people did Mrs. Davis have to pair me with Wes?

Maybe if I sent her an e-mail asking for a new partner, she'd agree to it. She seemed reasonable enough. But then I'd be causing problems on my first day. That seemed like a bad way to start off with a new teacher. But the thought of working with Wes made my stomach twist.

I thought about what Maby had said about him as I walked out of the classroom. Was there more to Wes than what met the eye?

"I guess it's just you and me." His voice drifted over my shoulder as he walked up behind me.

"I guess." I forced myself to turn and face him. "Or we could just each do our own poems and say that we worked on them together."

"Fi!" He gasped. "That would be dishonest, wouldn't it?" He fluttered his long dark lashes. "I could never do something like that."

"Sure." I looked down at my shoes, then back up at him. "I think it would be best if we did it that way."

"I disagree." He leaned against the locker beside me and stared into my eyes. "I want you, Fi—all to myself."

His smooth voice made my skin tingle. His words made my muscles tighten.

"I'm going to ask the teacher to switch me to a different partner." I turned away from him.

"Hey." He caught my hand and tugged me back. "What are you so scared of?" He smiled as he met my eyes. "I was just playing around. It was just for fun."

"I'm not having fun." I pulled my hand away and crossed my arms. "I'm not scared of you, Wes, if that's what you think. I just don't think we could work together. You should be paired up with someone else."

"I'm all you've got." He spread his arms wide. "Take me or leave me, but if we don't work together, I guarantee you Mrs. Davis will fail you."

The word "fail" sent a shiver down my spine. I couldn't allow my first graded assignment to be a failure. More than any other student, I needed to prove that I deserved to be here.

"Fine." I took a deep breath. "We can meet in the common room tonight to go over the assignment."

"I'll be there." He smirked as he met my eyes. "I'm looking forward to getting to know all your darkest secrets, Fi."

"Sure, just try to come up with something more emotionally intricate than whatever you did with that girl in the small library." I rolled my eyes, then turned and walked away from him.

"You've been spying on me, Fi?" he called after me and laughed.

My cheeks burned with heat as I quickened my pace to get away from him faster.

For the remainder of my classes I found it impossible to concentrate on much of what the teachers said. Instead, my thoughts kept wandering back to Wes's stupid laugh. Every time I thought of it, it made my body tense.

After the last bell for the day, I considered my options. Was there a way around this? Maybe I could find someone to trade partners with me and leave the teacher out of it. But I hadn't made any friends in the class yet. The other students seemed friendly enough, but they already had their friends to talk to and didn't need to include me.

I peeked into the common room. It was crowded with people. But none of them was Wes. Relieved, I walked through the space and into the hallway that led to the girls' dormitory. Maybe if I got my poem done first, it would make things easier. Then I would just have to endure helping him with his.

I settled on my bed and began reading over the material again.

Mrs. Davis had mentioned wanting to feel emotions in the poem.

As I read through some of the poetry, I could visualize the pain, the heartbreak, the determination that the poems portrayed. I'd had some of that in my life, though I preferred not to focus on it.

I set down the tablet and settled at my desk instead. As I began to scrawl some words onto paper, each one seemed to hang heavily from the line. I wrote about my absent father by describing the empty spaces in my life. The ball that sat in the grass, never tossed to me. The father-daughter dance fliers that I always passed to the kid behind me in class. But each word I used only made the situation seem more distant, more unreal.

Was that what really caused me pain?

I balled up the paper and tossed it into the trash can. I started a new poem about my excitement to be at Oak Brook Academy. I described the education I longed for, the opportunities I would have as a result of my attendance, and even the hope that I would make some lasting friendships.

As I read it over, it seemed as if my words were lost in a wind tunnel, with nothing to pin them down. Yes, they were grouped together, yes, they described an emotion, but they didn't have any real meaning.

I balled the paper up and tossed it into the trash.

As I sat back in my chair and closed my eyes, the chimes that indicated it was time for dinner rang out. Immediately, I was flooded with a memory of clutching to my favorite stuffed animal as a fire alarm blared. I held onto it so tight, because I already knew what it was like to lose something and never get it back.

My mind spun from the impact of the memory.

"Fi?" Maby knocked on my bedroom door. "Are you coming to dinner?"

My chest ached from the pounding of my heart. I drew a slow and shaky breath as I got to my feet. Had that even happened? I felt so young in the memory. My mother did tell me that there was a fire in one of the apartment buildings we'd lived in when I was young, but I'd never remembered it before.

"I'm coming." My hand curved around the cool doorknob. I took another slow breath and pushed the memory from my mind.

"I thought you were never coming out of there." Maby's dark eyes raked over mine as she crossed her arms. "I figured you must be busy."

"Just working on an assignment." I shook my head. "I got a little caught up in it."

"Oh, Wes told me about that." She quirked an eyebrow. "He said you couldn't wait to work with him. But I know better than that."

"Wes." I frowned. "He's the last person I would ever want to work with."

"I know that he's given you a pretty bad impression so far, but he's not as terrible as he seems." She pulled open the door to the hallway.

"Do you really believe that or are you saying that just because he's your friend?" I followed her out into the hall.

"He wouldn't be my friend if he was a terrible person. I know we probably all seem a little stuck up to you—spoiled, maybe even lazy. But Apple, Candy, Mick, Wes, and I—we're all friends for a reason. And now you're our friend too." She brushed some of my hair back behind my shoulder. "Trust me, if Wes is willing to work on a school project, it's because he actually wants to spend time with you."

As we reached the door to the cafeteria she paused, then met my eyes. "Just be careful, Fi. Wes is like a brother to me, but he has his problems and I don't want to see you caught up in them." She pulled open the door and stepped inside.

I let the door swing closed behind her. The haunted look in her eyes made me uneasy. One minute she praised Wes, the next she warned me against him. What wasn't she telling me?

NINE

When I joined the others at the table, everyone was already there. Everyone but Wes. I glanced around the cafeteria but saw no sign of him.

"Can I have that?" Mick pointed at the potato on my plate.

"Uh, sure." I smiled as he picked it up.

"Hot!" He laughed and tossed it between his hands.

"Shocking." Apple grinned.

"Hush!" Mick dropped the potato on his plate right next to his own. "According to Coach, I have to eat more if I'm going to bulk up before the college scouts show up."

"Oak Brook is not exactly known for athletics." Candy looked over at him with a wry smile. "Do you really think any scouts are going to be coming here?"

"We play Thompson next week. The scouts might show up there." Mick shrugged.

"Show up to watch you lose." Maby laughed. Then she ducked as Mick threw a balled-up napkin at her. "I'm sorry! You're a great player, Mick—you know that—but it takes a whole team to win a game."

"Don't remind me." He grunted, then dug into his potato.

"Is Wes on the football team too?" I thought about the way he'd held the football when I'd first met him.

"Ha! Wes on the team?" Mick chuckled. "Not much chance of that. He doesn't like to follow rules."

"Wes has issues with authority." Candy nodded. "He doesn't like to be told what to do."

"He's also not very fit." Mick mumbled around his mouthful of potato.

"Yes, there's that." Maby grinned.

I dug into my chicken and thought about meeting Wes after dinner. If he hadn't shown up for dinner, would he show up for our meeting? Again I scanned the cafeteria for any sign of him. Was he sitting with one of his girlfriends?

"Where is Wes anyway?" Maby finally asked the question.

"Oh, he got a phone call." Apple cringed. "Haven't seen him since."

"Ah." Maby's voice dropped. She piled some food into her mouth and looked away from me.

I waited, hoping that the others at the table would discuss the phone call further. Instead, everyone became very quiet.

"So, what else do you guys do around here on the weekend? Do we have to stick around or are we allowed to go out and explore?"

"You have to get permission from Mrs. Reed and usually she insists that we go everywhere in groups of three or more." Candy shrugged. "But other than that, we can go wherever we want. Well, not the younger grades, but the juniors and seniors can."

"Into the city?" I smiled at the idea. "There are so many things I want to see."

"Well aren't you an adorable little tourist?" Maby pinched my cheek. "Don't tell me you've never been to New York City before."

I pushed her hand away and smiled. "Okay, I won't tell you."

"She's a virgin?" Mick shouted as he jumped up from his chair.

The entire cafeteria went silent and all eyes turned toward our table.

"Mick!" Apple smacked his arm. "What have I told you about your outbursts? Have you asked the nurse to up your meds?"

"I just meant that she's a New York City virgin." He furrowed an eyebrow as he sat back down. "Why? What did I say that was so wrong?"

"Mick." Maby rolled her eyes and rested her head against her hands.

"Wow." Candy burst out laughing. "I guess the whole school is going to be even more curious about you now, Fi." She winked at me.

I had never felt my cheeks burn so hot. As mortified as I was, I couldn't help but find it funny too. Just the look on Mick's face was enough to make me laugh.

"Yes, Mick, I'm a New York City virgin." I grinned. "I can't wait to check out all the sights!"

"Ugh, we've been to all of them a dozen times at least." Apple scrunched up her nose. "They call them field trips."

"That's true but Fi hasn't been here for those trips." Maby draped her arm over my shoulder. "Don't worry, we'll get you there."

"Great." As I left the cafeteria my spirits were a little brighter. Even though Mick had embarrassed me, I felt as if I had some real friends for the first time in my life.

It wasn't until I stepped into the common room that I even remembered that I was supposed to meet with Wes. Determined to get through it and not let it bother me, I settled on one of the sofas and opened up my backpack. I smiled to myself at the thought of Maby's giving it to me.

With my tablet and notebook in my lap, I began writing about seeing some of the sights in New York City.

An hour slipped by.

I stood up and rubbed the back of my neck, then stretched my arms above my head. Then I sat back down and began to write some more.

Another hour slipped by.

The common room emptied out until I was the only one still there. In the quiet, empty room I glanced at my watch again. He hadn't even bothered to show up.

I sighed as I started to put my things away.

When the door swung open, I glanced up, not expecting it to be him.

Wes froze in the doorway, as if he hadn't expected to see me either.

"You're still here?" His usual half-smile had been replaced by a tense frown.

"I was supposed to meet someone here to work on a project." I shrugged. "I showed up, he didn't."

"Sorry." He shoved his hands into his pockets. "I had something going on."

"Oh, okay." I watched as his hair fell into his eyes and his lips pursed. "Well, this assignment is important. You might not care about your grades, but I care about mine. If you don't want to do it, then tell me now and I'll figure out how to get it done without you."

"That simple, right?" He tossed his hair out of his face and glared at me. "Like I don't even exist?"

"You're the one that didn't show up." I took a slight step back as he suddenly crossed the room in my direction.

"Like I said, I had something going on." He stopped right in front of me and stared straight into my eyes.

"Something," I mumbled, unsettled by how close he was. "Something that made you stay out until you thought I wouldn't be here?"

"Yes." He raised an eyebrow. "So?"

"So, I was here because you said you would meet me." I crossed my arms in an attempt to create more distance between us.

"I'm here now." His arm glided along mine as he brushed past me and plopped down on the sofa. "Let's do it."

"Now?" I turned around to face him. "Isn't there some kind of curfew?"

"We've got time." He looked up at me. "Do you want to do the assignment or not?"

I wanted to scream the word "no" right in his face. It burned on the tip of my tongue. But given his track record for not showing up, I guessed that this might be my best chance to actually get the assignment done.

"Fine." I sat down on the sofa beside him with plenty of space between us. "Do you know what you want to write about?"

"I guess." He picked at the material of his jeans stretched taut over his knee.

"Okay, do you have your notebook?" I looked over his t-shirt and jeans and didn't wait for an answer. "Here." I tore a few pages out of my notebook and handed them to him. "I guess you need a pen too?" I pulled one out of my backpack and held it out to him.

He met my eyes as he took it. But instead of pulling the pen free of my grasp, he closed his hand over mine and pinned the pen in place.

"I'm going to write about you. I'm going to write about that judgmental look in your eyes."

"What?" I rolled my eyes. "You're the one that showed up late and unprepared."

"And you're the one that doesn't care why." He pulled the pen free and looked down at the notebook paper piled up on his knee. "Pretty cold, don't you think, Fi?"

TEN

His words stung. A little because they were infuriating and a little because they weren't wrong. It was clear to see that something had Wes upset, but my focus was only on getting our assignment done. Maybe he hadn't been a good friend to me so far, but that didn't mean I couldn't at least try to reach out to him.

"Do you want to talk about it?" I turned on the sofa so that I could face him.

"Nope." He ran the pen along the paper in a long squiggly line.

"Do you want to write about it?" I tried to meet his eyes, but with his head tipped forward, his hair hid them from me.

"Not a chance." He drew a deep breath, then looked at me. "I'll tell you what. Why don't you write my poem for me?"

"Me?" I stared at him. "How can I possibly do that? I don't know anything about you."

"No, you don't. But I think you've already made up your mind about me. So write it." He offered me the pen back. "I'm curious. What will it say?"

"We don't have time to play games, Wes." I frowned and

looked back at my notebook. "I'll just get to work on mine. You do what you want."

"I told you what I want." His hand came to rest on my knee with the pen still grasped in it. "Go on, write about me. I'll write about you."

"That's crazy." I looked up at him in the same moment that I pushed his hand away. "You certainly don't know a single thing about me. It's just a waste of time."

"Aren't you curious?" He raised an eyebrow and smiled. "What do you think I'll write about you?"

"Have you been drinking?" I peered closely at him. Something about the easy way he talked, his constant amusement at my reactions, and the general lack of care in his attitude made me think he had to be at least a little tipsy.

"I don't drink." He shot me a sharp look. "But maybe you should include that in your poem about me."

"You want me to write a poem about you?" I glared at him. "Fine, I'll write a poem about you. Then can we move on to the actual assignment?"

"Fine." He smiled and shrugged. "Sounds good to me."

I shook my head, then focused on filling the paper with exactly what I thought about him. I wrote about his coldness, his lazy attitude, and his disrespectful tone. I wrote about how irritating he was and how I couldn't wait to finish the assignment.

When I glanced over at him, I noticed the way he scrawled words across his paper. He wrote with big letters that ignored the guidance of the lines.

Just one more way he rebelled.

As I watched him stare hard at the paper—his lips taut, his eyes shadowed by thick lashes—I began to wonder. What was it about him that made him so determined not to care? Not to listen?

A few strands of his hair tumbled out from behind his ear

and settled against the curve of his cheek. My fingers itched to reach up and tuck it back.

Horrified, I gripped my pen tighter and looked back at my notebook. As I read over my scathing words, I began to see myself through his eyes.

He was right about the judgment, wasn't he? I'd written down about twenty different labels for him. Sure, they seemed accurate, but how could I know for sure?

I glanced back at him and my eyes collided with his.

"Done?" His lips relaxed into that easy smile that indicated he knew all the secrets of the universe.

"Not yet." I stared back at him. For once, I didn't flinch and look away. Instead, I stared straight into his eyes, past that glazed look of superiority, past the hint of amusement that surfaced every time he looked in my direction.

Who was there—behind all those defenses?

I turned back to my paper and added a few more lines to it. Then I nodded. "I'm done now."

"Me too." He held out his paper to me.

"Here." I tore out the paper from my notebook and handed it to him as I took his in my other hand.

"See you tomorrow." He stood up and headed for the hall that led to the boys' dormitory.

"What?" I stood up as well. "What about the assignment?"

"Done!" He turned back and grinned at me. "I've got a poem I can turn in. I'm sure it'll get a great grade."

"What about me?" I glared at him.

"You've got one too." He winked at me. "If you don't like it, you can always rewrite it."

The anger that rushed through me was so intense that I lost all control over my mouth.

"It's probably nothing but garbage! You don't take anything seriously!"

"Garbage." He nodded as he stared into my eyes for a long moment, then he turned and continued to walk away.

I thought about chasing after him. I thought about demanding that he work with me. But what would be the point of that? The whole thing had been a charade just to get me to do his work for him. I could see that now. He had a poem about himself that he could turn in and the teacher would probably think it was amazingly honest and emotional.

Me, on the other hand, what did I have?

I guessed that he'd probably written "Ha-ha, you idiot" on my paper.

Furious, I shoved everything into my backpack and stormed back to my dorm room. If there was one thing I was sure of, it was that I never wanted to so much as look at him again.

When I threw the door open, Maby gasped and jumped up from the sofa.

"Fi? What's wrong?"

"I don't care what you say about Wes, he is a jerk!" I scowled at her, then marched into my room. I would have slammed the door if I didn't think that it might get me in trouble. Instead, I tossed my backpack on my bed and flopped down beside it. "Stupid Wes."

I closed my eyes tight and tried not to think about that embarrassing moment when I thought about touching his hair.

What was wrong with me? Why, after seventeen years of barely noticing the cute boys in the hallway, did this particular boy keep popping up in my mind?

Tears of frustration slipped down my cheeks. I'd come to Oak Brook wanting nothing more than stability, some friendship, and a great education. So far, I felt more unstable than I ever had in the dank, dirty apartments I'd lived in.

Maby claimed to be my friend, but was she just teasing me like Wes?

As for the education, I was sure that Mrs. Davis would see straight through anything I tried to write and realize that I hadn't actually done the assignment as she'd asked.

A fresh rush of anger drove me to my feet. No, I wouldn't let him win. I wouldn't lose everything I'd hoped for just because of Wes playing his usual games.

I pulled my notebook out of my backpack and flipped it open on my desk. As I did, the paper he'd handed me slipped out and fell to the floor. I looked down at the shredded edges of the notebook paper and the too-large letters that he'd scrawled across it.

My fingers trembled as they closed around the flimsy paper —out of anger—surely.

At least that's what I told myself as I sat down at my desk and began to read what he'd written.

ELEVEN

Sophie

STARLIGHT HIDDEN by the clouds
she won't whisper she won't shout
she won't say a word out loud,
but nothing can shut that light out.
I can see it glowing,
as she hides behind her fear.
I can see it growing,
as she tries her hardest to disappear.
Beauty like that, doesn't need make-up,
it doesn't need a fancy dress,
it doesn't ever have to be touched-up.
It's a perfect, exquisite, total mess.
She thinks she can fade away,
she can always find a place to hide,
but when she's got something to say,
she just can't keep it inside.
Yell at me, gorgeous, as loud as you can,

if it means I get to hear your voice.
But if you ever try to hide again,
I won't let you make that choice.
I
see
you
Fi.

THE PAPER SLIPPED OUT of my hand and fell right back to the floor. As I stared down at it, I could hear the pounding of my heartbeat echoing throughout my body.

How had a boy like Wes just written something so powerful about me? It was as if he had taken a long swim through every experience I'd ever had. Yes, it was always safer to hide. But did he really see the things he claimed? Did he find me beautiful? Or was that just something he wrote to lure me in?

I sank down on the edge of the bed and closed my eyes. Just for a moment, I let myself believe that he meant every word.

Shock raced through my mind, then a warmth—a kind of demanding warmth that I'd never felt before. As it grew, I realized it was a need. I wished he was right there beside me so that I could take his hand and look into his eyes and see the truth.

I jumped up from my bed and shivered. No, I'd never felt anything so powerful.

I tried to ignore it, but his writing stared up at me from the floor. When I bent down to pick up the paper again, I tried to convince myself that I didn't understand what I'd read. He couldn't have really meant those things the way that I'd taken them. There had to be some other explanation.

I thought about the words I'd written down on his paper, the terrible way that I'd described him. Yes, at the end, I wrote down what I truly saw, but that didn't change what I'd written in the first place.

Had he read it?

I winced and hoped that he'd crumpled it up and thrown it away. With my stomach in knots I began to panic. What if he did read it?

I pulled open my bedroom door and stepped out into the living room. "Maby!"

"Oh, you're talking to me now?" She turned to look at me from where she sat on the sofa.

"Please. I need Wes's number. You have it, don't you?" I joined her on the sofa.

"Sure. But why do you need it?" She narrowed her eyes. "Fi, are you okay? You look upset."

"I am upset." I sighed. "Please, just tell me his number. I have to send him a message as soon as possible."

"I'm not so sure that's a good idea with the way you're acting." She raised an eyebrow. "Did something happen tonight? Did he take things too far?"

"No." I frowned and clenched my hands into fists. "But I think maybe that I did. Please, I've done something terrible and I need to send him a text before he realizes it."

"Okay, okay." She pulled out her phone. "Here's his number." She handed me the phone with his contact info pulled up.

"Thanks."

As I typed it into my phone, my fingers trembled.

As soon as it was in, I began typing out a text to him.

IT'S SOPHIE. Please throw away the poem I wrote. Don't read it, don't even look at it.

. . .

I HIT SEND BEFORE I could talk myself out of it.

Maybe he'd already thrown it away. If he was the kind of person I had first assumed he was, he probably had tossed it in the nearest trash can.

But that person didn't write poems like the one he'd written for me. That person, I was beginning to realize—the person I first believed Wes to be—might not even exist.

"Now, are you going to tell me what's going on?" Maby took my hand and looked into my eyes. "I'm your friend, Fi, I'm here for you. You can tell me what happened. If he did something to hurt you, I'll be the first one in line to knock some sense into him."

"No, he didn't do anything like that." I stared at the screen on my phone. Would he text me back? Would he confirm that he hadn't read the poem? "We were working on something together and I got upset with him. He wanted us to write poems about each other, so I did, but I wasn't kind." I bit into my bottom lip, then shook my head. "That isn't true. I was cruel. I've never said things like that about anyone before."

"Relax, I'm sure it's nothing that Wes hasn't heard before." She draped her arm over my shoulder. "He's got thick skin. I can't believe that he actually wrote a poem, though."

"I thought he did it to get me to write one for him that he could turn in to the teacher. But when I read what he wrote..." My cheeks grew hot. "Well, it just wasn't what I expected."

"Wes can really surprise you." Maby pursed her lips, then looked straight into my eyes. "Maybe it's time I told you a little bit more about him."

"Yes, I'd like that." I checked my phone again. Still no response. But why would he respond to a text like that? I had no idea if he'd received it or if he would honor my request. I turned my attention to Maby as she continued.

"Wes has had it easy in a lot of ways. His dad has tons of

money. I mean, more money probably than anyone else who attends this school. He owns several businesses. Wes has had everything he ever wanted handed to him, but he's also had a father that is constantly away. His mom died when he was only eight and after that he had nothing but nannies." She raised an eyebrow. "With his issues with authority, you can only imagine how that's gone, right?"

"Right." I thought about my own father's absence. No, my mother hadn't been any kind of gem, but at least I'd had her.

"He went through a parade of nannies until his father put him in boarding school. Most of us here started in junior high or high school. Wes has been attending boarding schools since he was ten." She shook her head. "He and his father don't get along at all. If Wes ever gets a chance to see him, it's usually because he's in trouble for something."

"The phone call tonight?" I met her eyes. "Do you think it was his father?"

"I'm sure it was. Whenever Wes gets a call, he disappears for a while. He has to blow off some steam. So, yes, he's had every material thing he could ever want, but you and I both know that's not all that's needed." She tipped her head to the side. "Sure, I love a new pair of shoes, but I'd trade them in for a spa day with my mom any day."

"I know what you mean." I frowned. I didn't, exactly. I had no urge to spend time with my mother. In fact, I'd already gotten used to the idea of being away from her. But I could imagine what Maby meant. More than that, I could imagine what Wes must be going through. He was right, I had judged him from the start. Sure, the way he acted wasn't great, but clearly his attitude hid a lot of pain. "I'm sorry he's been through so much."

"We all have." She tipped her head to the side. "Some more than others. But I guess when it comes down to it, you and Wes aren't that different. Now tell me the truth, what did he do that really upset you?"

I stared back at her, unsure how to answer.

What had he done?

He'd seen me.

"Nothing, it was nothing."

TWELVE

I spent most of the night checking my phone and rereading the poem.

When I finally fell asleep, my alarm went off just a few hours later. I woke up with a jolt and reached for my phone again.

Still no messages.

I scrolled through my recent calls and messages. Maybe my service wasn't working. My mother usually texted me at least once a day and I hadn't heard from her either. She hadn't called to ask how my first day was. No matter where we landed in life, she did always make an effort to check in with me. So where was she?

I decided to call her—something I rarely did—just to make sure my service worked. The phone rang several times before it went to voicemail. I hung up before it asked me to leave me a message. Strange.

The thought was pushed from my mind by the reality I faced. During my first class of the day, I was going to see Wes. Whether he had gotten my text or not, whether he had read the poem or not, I was going to see him.

I couldn't even imagine looking at him after what he'd written about me. As insightful as it was, as kind as it was, I knew better than to expect it to be true. He likely had just made it up to string me along. Or maybe to tease me. Either way, he would know that he had written it and he would assume that I'd read it.

What would I say to him?

I decided the best thing to do was not to speak.

Luckily, I had a chance to practice. Maby sat across from me in our small kitchen and had a lot to say.

"So, I've arranged our first sight-seeing trip this weekend. Mrs. Reed approved all of us to go. First thing you should see is Lady Liberty, of course." She smiled. "What do you think?"

"That sounds great." I finished the last of my toast. "I'm really excited about it. You, me, Apple, Candy, and Mick?"

"And Wes. Of course." She winked at me. "Don't worry, I'll keep you two separated."

"Great." I sighed. Even the thought of being with him in a classroom for forty-five minutes seemed like an eternity. Would I survive a day trip with him?

I checked my phone one last time as I walked toward my first class. No text from Wes and nothing from my mother either. With my nerves on edge, I stepped through the door into the classroom. Just about every desk was taken, but two sat empty at the back of the room.

My heart skipped a beat as I wondered if I'd made Wes angry enough not to show up for class. The things I'd said in the poem flashed through my mind.

I settled at my desk and did my best to keep my eyes on the tablet in front of me. I listened—not to the voice of the teacher as she began to speak—but for the sound of the door opening. I held my breath as seconds continued to slip by.

Then I heard it—the slow and subtle squeak, the light click of the latch as the door fell closed.

I looked up just as Mrs. Davis turned to look at Wes.

"Class starts at the same time each day, Wesley—for everyone."

"Right." He nodded to her, but his eyes settled on me.

I willed myself to look away, but his heavy gaze seemed to trap mine and hold it as he walked toward me.

He paused beside my desk, his lips twitched upward into a faint smirk. As he sat down, he leaned close to me as if he might say something, but instead, he sat back and let his hair fall into his eyes.

I opened my mouth to say something—anything.

"Sophie?"

"Huh?" I turned to the front of the classroom and found that just about everyone had their attention on me, including Mrs. Davis.

"How is your project coming along?" Mrs. Davis smiled as she walked down the aisle toward me. "I know it can be a lot to ask and not necessarily what you're used to."

"Oh, it's fine." I cleared my throat.

"Great. And Wes?" She looked over at him. "Are you making yourself available to Sophie?"

A few of the other students made unsuccessful attempts to muffle their laughter.

"I'm all hers." Wes quirked a smile as he looked at the teacher. "I plan to teach her everything I know."

Several more students laughed and this time they didn't attempt to hide it.

"What's the joke?" Mrs. Davis glanced around at the other students.

I knew what the joke was. Everyone in the class knew about Wes's reputation. He didn't spend time with girls for no reason.

He flirted and teased, drawing them into his web. To the rest of the students in the class, I was just his latest prey.

I looked down at my tablet again as my heart pounded. Had I been conned? Were the words that he'd written meaningless?

"I don't know what the issue is here, but Sophie is a new student. We're going to welcome her, right?" Mrs. Davis shot sharp looks at students who dared to continue to laugh. When she looked back at me, I noticed a hint of apology in her eyes. "Sophie, if there's a problem, I can switch you to a different partner."

There it was. Everything I had hoped for since the first moment that Wes and I had been paired up. The opportunity to be rid of him.

I didn't have to look over at him to know that his eyes were on me. I could feel the weight of them.

I had no idea what I wanted. But what did he want? Did he want to be rid of me too?

My instincts told me to just switch partners and be done with it. It had turned into a big mess anyway. But the thought of doing it made my breath catch in my throat. What if I never found out the truth about why he'd written the poem?

"No, it's fine. No problem." I sat back in my chair as she smiled.

I didn't dare to look over at Wes. I didn't want to see that stupid knowing smile that made him king of the world. I didn't want to find a scowl on his face, showing his annoyance at me for not solving our problem when I had the opportunity to. I didn't want to exist at all. I wished I could melt right into the floor.

Mrs. Davis continued on with the class, but I couldn't focus on a single word she said. I'd come to Oak Brook Academy for the stellar education, and now, all I could think about was the boy sitting next to me. How had that happened?

The more I thought about it, the angrier I felt.

It was his fault, after all. He didn't have to write that poem. He didn't have to be my partner in the project. He had slithered into my brain and twisted up all my thoughts. He had done what I didn't think was even possible.

I forced myself to glance over in his direction. He had an app open on his tablet—some kind of video game. His eyes remained on that. Of course he wasn't paying attention. Of course he was breaking the rules. Why did I expect anything else?

I jumped up from my seat the moment that class ended. I couldn't get out of there fast enough as I pushed past the other students, whose names and faces I still didn't remember. They only knew who I was because I was Wes's partner—because I had his attention, even in the smallest way. Other than that, I was still nothing to them.

I was the first one out the door and into the busy hallway. Instead of heading to my next class, I headed for the main door. I needed air—desperately.

I needed to be somewhere that he wasn't.

THIRTEEN

I pushed through the door that led out into the courtyard and sucked down a few breaths of the morning air. Thick clouds muted the sunlight, painting everything gray, as if the day refused to truly start.

I wished it hadn't.

Oak Brook Academy was supposed to be a place where I would have the chance to find myself, but I'd never felt more lost in my life.

I sat down on a stone bench and closed my eyes. If I could just get myself to calm down—if I could just turn back into the Sophie that never had a problem controlling my emotions—then maybe I could get through the rest of the day.

I took another deep breath and imagined myself somewhere quiet, surrounded by nothing but trees. Yes, like that one place my mom and I had lived when she was in love with a hunter. His house backed up to the woods, and at ten, I spent most of my time among the trees. It was beautiful—until the day I heard the first gunshot.

"Fi."

His voice cracked through my imagination as loud and

disruptive as the sounds of the shotgun that had made me flee from the woods all those years ago.

My heart raced as I tried to find a way to escape, to slip away before he got any closer. But I felt his warmth, too close to avoid. The next deep breath I took was laced with the spicy-smooth scent of his cologne.

When had that become such a delicious smell to me?

Maybe if I just kept my eyes closed.

I felt him sit down on the bench next to me. I opened my eyes enough to see his hands on his knees and the way his jeans hugged his legs until they reached the tops of his shoes.

Yes, he was there alright. I could run away, but it wouldn't solve anything. He would still be there, tangled up in the strangest emotions I'd ever felt.

"You didn't text me back." I blurted out the words. They had nothing to do with what I actually wanted to say.

"I know." He shifted on the bench beside me.

I didn't take my eyes off his hands on his knees. His finger-tips wriggled just a little bit against the material, making small circles as if he was trying to stay calm.

"I'm going to be late for class." I stood up, though my muscles threatened to give way in the process. It was as if even my body had turned against the idea of walking away from him.

"Fi." His hand caught mine before I could even think of pulling it away. He gave it a firm tug and pulled me back down onto the bench beside him. "It doesn't have to be like this."

"Yes, it does." I finally looked at his face, only to find it half-hidden by his hair. He knew how to hide when he wanted to. "Why did you write that about me, Wes? Why? Did you just want to see how I would react?"

"What?" He brushed his hair away from his eyes as he looked at me. "Is that what you think?"

"Why did you write it?" I stared into his eyes, determined not to be intimidated or lost in their deep shade of green.

"Why did you write this?" He held up the poem I'd written as he stared back at me.

"I'm sorry." I looked down at my own hands. My fingertips had dug through the fabric of my pants and beyond that into my skin. I had to find a way to stay calm. "I never should have written those things about you. I was just angry and I—"

"You didn't mean any of it?" He stood up from the bench and turned to face me. "Is that what you're saying?"

I looked up at him just as the sun began to burn past the heavy clouds. For a moment everything appeared to be edged in gold, then I had to squint as my eyes watered in response to the sudden blast of sunlight.

"Did you? Did you mean what you wrote?" My muscles pulsed in anticipation of what his response might be.

"It doesn't matter, does it?" He shook his head and turned away. "You'd better get to class. You wouldn't want to get into trouble."

I watched as he walked away. I clenched my teeth as I resisted the urge to go after him. No longer did I just see some smug boy that didn't think further than his own pleasure. I saw a boy who had lost his mother, been abandoned by his father, and maybe a boy who felt just as lost as I did most days.

I went through the motions of the remainder of my classes before lunch, but I still had a hard time focusing.

Our conversation hung over my head as I walked into the lunchroom.

When Wes arrived, he barely looked at me. He joked with the others at the table, then took off without saying a word directly to me.

Maby walked up to me as I was leaving the cafeteria.

"What's going on with the two of you?" She frowned as she fell into step beside me.

"What do you mean?" I glanced over at her.

"After what you told me this morning and then the way he acted at lunch, something isn't right." She shook her head.

"What do you mean the way he acted? He seemed pretty normal to me."

"Are you kidding?" She laughed. "He stared at you the whole time. You didn't notice?"

"He barely looked at me." I narrowed my eyes.

"You must have been looking away the whole time, because he had his eyes on you. Fi, I'm really glad you're my friend." She gave me a quick hug, then left her hands on my shoulders as she looked into my eyes. "But Wes, he doesn't need any more drama than he already has. He might act like nothing gets to him, but that's not who he really is."

"I'm starting to see that." I frowned. "Are you worried I'm going to hurt him?"

"I'm just saying that I've never seen him look at anyone like that before." She gave my shoulders a light squeeze, then turned and walked away.

I leaned back against a nearby locker and did my best to get my thoughts together. Not that long ago, Maby was worried about me and now she was worried that I would hurt Wes? I didn't think it was possible for someone like me to hurt someone like him.

My stomach flipped as I thought about the words he'd written. What if he meant every one of them? What if he really thought that I meant the terrible things I'd said about him?

I wasn't sure what I could do to fix things, but I knew that I had to find a way and fast.

Not only did I want to redeem myself, but I wanted to be able to actually concentrate on my education. Maybe if I apologized, we could straighten everything out and move on. Wes could go back to being Wes and I could go back to being invisible—and everything would be just fine.

Determined to do just that, I pulled out my phone.

I'M sorry for the things I wrote about you. I shouldn't have written them.

I STARTED to type more but deleted the extra words. I needed to keep it simple. I needed things to not be so messy. I needed the thought of him leaning close to me to not make me feel dizzy and weak. I had never been controlled by my emotions before and I wasn't about to start now.

For the rest of the day I checked my phone after every class.

Nothing. Not a single word.

Couldn't he at least send a thumbs up? An emoji with its tongue sticking out? Was that too much to ask?

By the time I returned to my dorm room, I'd convinced myself that he knew he was torturing me and that he was enjoying it. It wasn't as if I didn't deserve it after the things I'd written.

I gave up on hearing from him and focused on my homework.

About halfway through math, my phone buzzed with a text.

I snatched it up.

"It's probably from Mom," I muttered.

But it was his name that showed on the screen, followed by his words.

FOURTEEN

Meet me in the courtyard.

NOT A WORD ABOUT MY APOLOGY. Not a word about how he felt. Just a demand for me to be face-to-face with him.

Did I want to do that?

I looked down at my half-completed math homework. I had things to do. I had reasons to say that I couldn't meet him.

Another text came through seconds later.

WE HAVE a project to work on, remember? It's due on Thursday.

YES, I remembered. In fact, it had been weighing on my mind quite a bit.

As I stared at the words on the screen, I knew it was the only way to get back on track. I had to get him off my mind, so I could get my mind back on the things that mattered—my classes and making Oak Brook Academy work for me.

I sent him a quick text in return, letting him know that I'd be there in a few minutes. As I walked past the mirror that hung over the dresser, I caught sight of my limp hair and my pale skin.

How could he ever describe me as gorgeous? I was kidding myself to even consider it. Wes had his choice of girls on campus, that was clear. He didn't need to bother himself with someone as plain and unimportant as me.

I reminded myself of that as I stepped out into the courtyard. Maybe he had written the poem out of kindness, but that didn't mean he felt that way about me. I needed to keep my head on straight and stop giving in to fantasies.

As I walked through the courtyard, I didn't see any sign of him. Had he just lured me out here to be a no-show again?

"Fi, over here." He waved to me from behind one of the stone statues in the courtyard.

Behind it was a bench in a little enclave, set back from the rest of the courtyard. I'd never noticed it before.

He walked over to the bench and sat down. I noticed that he had a notebook and a pen with him this time.

He looked up at me and patted the bench beside him. "Let's get to work."

I knew it was now or never. I had to get the apology over with so that I could concentrate on our project.

"Wes, I just want to say that I'm sorry about what I wrote." I frowned as he met my eyes. "I'm not usually so cruel and it was really unfair of me to say those things about you."

"Those things?" He smirked and pulled a folded piece of paper out of his notebook.

As he unfolded it, I realized what it was.

My heart slammed against my chest as he stood up from the bench and walked toward me.

"'Vain. It's so good to be so pretty.'" he glanced up at me and smiled. "'Callous. No one else matters but me.'"

"Wes, don't. I said I was sorry." I took a step back.

He crossed the distance I created and continued. "'Cruel. I take pleasure in creating misery. No one can touch me, nothing can hurt me. I'm as slippery as slippery can be.'" He chuckled as he lowered the paper for a moment. "That line was a little sing-songy, I thought—like the good doctor we all read as kids?"

"I'm sorry." My face flushed with heat and I inched back again, right into the statue behind me.

"Why are you sorry?" He locked his eyes to mine. "For being honest?"

"I was just angry, I didn't mean any of that." I licked my lips as he drew closer to me.

Could he sense my fear? My embarrassment? Having my own words spoken back to me made them even harder to deny.

"None of it?" He lifted the paper between us again. "Not even this part? 'But it's all just for show, though nobody may ever know that I act like a fool just to make myself look cool. No matter how good it seems on the outside, I'm all alone inside.'" He glanced up at me just for a moment, then looked back down at the paper. "'I'll laugh in your face and ask for nothing but space, while the me that no one gets to see keeps weeping—hasn't been sleeping.'" He took a slow breath, then continued with the last two lines. "'So alone and lost in my greatest fear. I'll be gone before anyone knows I was here.'" He folded the paper back up, then looked into my eyes.

I couldn't look away. There was nowhere for me to hide, with the statue against my back and his face inches from mine.

"Do you think I'm alone, Fi?" He smiled a little. "I've got more friends than anyone else here. If I want company, all I have to do is ask. But this is how you see me?" He held the paper out to me.

It surprised me that he wasn't angry about my harsh words. Instead, he wanted to know about the words that had come to me when I'd finally truly looked at him. Hadn't I insulted him by describing him that way?

"It doesn't matter. We have work to do." I started to step around him.

"It does." His hand splayed against the curve of my waist and stopped my progress. He met my eyes as I looked up at him. "We're supposed to be honest, right?"

His hand lingered against my shirt.

The warmth of his palm emanated through the thin material and inspired my skin to tingle.

There it was again—that stupid fantasy that I'd been fighting against.

"I don't know anything about you, Wes." I took a breath as I dared to stare into his eyes. "I'm no one to you. Why do you care what I think?"

"I just want you to answer the question." He let his hand fall back to his side and took a small step back. "That's all."

"Yes." I felt some relief at the distance between us, but at the same time, it felt like a loss. "I think you're very alone."

He tipped his head to the side and smiled. His eyes gleamed with that hint of amusement. His hair tickled at his eyelashes, his broad shoulders spread even wider.

In that moment, he looked untouchable. But I knew better. I knew I wasn't wrong. After Maby had told me what she had, it made me even more certain that Wes had a lot to hide.

"And I don't think that you deserve to be."

He flinched, glancing away from me as he took a slow breath in.

"Well, I guess we have that in common. Don't we?" He looked back at me, then walked over to the bench and picked up his notebook. "We'd better make some progress if we're going to be done on time. I wouldn't want to be the callous, cruel person that gets you a bad grade." He flashed me a grin.

I had no idea how he could fluctuate so fast from serious to playful, but he'd made the transition look like nothing. As I sat down beside him, he suddenly leaned close to me and looked into my eyes.

"Fi?"

"Yes?" I took a sharp breath in reaction to his sudden closeness.

"Do you really think I'm pretty?" He batted his eyelashes at me.

"Wes!" I rolled my eyes and shoved him away as I laughed.

"I'm just asking." He smacked his lips together in a playful kiss, which only made me laugh harder.

The laughter broke the tension between us and soon we were working on our actual assignment. I noticed that when he focused, he had no problem working hard.

As I stole a look at him, I didn't feel any more certain about whether he'd meant what he'd said in the poem he'd written for me, but I wanted to know more about him.

Maybe he was a puzzle, but maybe he was one that I wanted to solve.

FIFTEEN

After a terrible night's sleep, I woke up with one thought on my mind.

My mother.

She still hadn't called or texted. Memories of the times I would have to hunt her down when things had gone wrong flooded over me. She didn't always—or mostly—make the best decisions, and often got herself into some terrible circumstances. What had happened this time?

Dale seemed like a nice enough guy—at least nicer than most of the men she'd dated—but then again, I'd only spoken to him a few times. I really hoped that for her sake—and mine—she hadn't done something to mess up their relationship.

I crawled out of bed, my mind still fuzzy from lack of sleep, and picked up my phone. As I dialed her number thoughts about the night before resurfaced in my mind.

I wished that I could share the way I felt with my mom— that I could talk through my confusion with her like I guessed other moms and daughters could. But if I even mentioned Wes, she would do everything in her power to embarrass me. She meant well, I guessed, but that didn't mean I could trust her.

The phone continued to ring.

I thought about Wes losing his mother at such a young age. That was a kind of grief that I doubted anyone could get over.

I sighed as her voicemail picked up yet again.

"Mom, what is going on? I haven't heard from you. Please call me back or text me. Just let me know that everything is okay." I hung up the phone and frowned. "She's probably just off on some fancy excursion without cell service." I imagined her sprawled out in a hammock in some tropical place that only rich people knew about.

I hoped that was the case, anyway.

With her still on my mind, I joined Maby for breakfast.

"Hey, you look rough." She quirked an eyebrow as she looked at me. "What happened to you last night?"

"I couldn't sleep." I shook my head and drew a deep breath. "Too much on my mind, I guess."

"Wes?" She cringed. "I heard the two of you were together in the courtyard."

"You did?" My eyes widened. I had no idea that anyone else had seen us.

"There are no secrets here, Fi." She grinned. "You can pass a note to a friend in first period and the entire school will know the contents of the note—why you wrote it and exactly what time you passed it—by the time you get to lunch."

"That's...disturbing." I laughed a little as I peeled the wrapper off a muffin.

"So it's true?" She picked up her glass of juice and took a sip.

"Yes, we were in the courtyard." My cheeks warmed at the memory of his hand on my waist.

"Doing what?" She took a bite of her muffin.

"Working on our project."

"Oh, is that what they call making out where you're from?"

She laughed. "Cute."

"What?" I laughed too. "No, we were not making out. We were working on our project for class. That's all. Are you kidding me?"

"I'm just trying to get the lay of the land before our plan for Saturday, that's all." She shrugged. "I mean, if you two are going to hook up, there's nothing I can do to stop you, but at least have the decency to tell me."

"No!" I nearly choked on my muffin.

"Oh, you don't like to kiss and tell?" She rolled her eyes.

"Maby!" I stared at her. "Look at me. Do you really think Wes would be interested in someone like me?"

"Girl, you may not be model material, but you have that mysterious edge that drives the boys wild." She took another bite of her muffin and wiggled her eyebrows.

"Now I know you've lost your mind." I laughed and tossed my empty wrapper at her. "Listen, I have never driven any boy wild and certainly not Wes."

"Okay, okay!" She laughed as she dodged the wrapper. "No need to attack!"

"Actually, though, you were right." I smiled as I rolled my glass of juice between my palms. "He's not so bad. I think we could even be friends. Eventually."

"That's progress." She nodded. "He sure does seem to like to be around you."

"Only because we're working on this project." I grabbed my backpack then finished the last of my juice. "I'll see you later, I've got some homework to catch up on before class."

"See you." Maby waved to me as I hurried out the door.

On my way to the classroom my own words came back to haunt me. It was true that once we turned in our project the next day, Wes would be a free man again. He wouldn't need to be around me. Would he still want to be? Certainly not if he discovered that I'd developed a crush on him. It didn't matter how strange I felt around him, I could never cross that line.

Wes could have anyone—and I thought that he did—without much care to what happened to them after. If I dared to even bring up the possibility of us being together, I would just be another check on his list of Oak Brook girls that he'd made swoon with those stupid green eyes that looked way too far into mine.

My thoughts wandered off for a second back to the night before—back to him standing so close to me.

"No!" I didn't realize I'd spoken the word out loud until a few students in the hallway gave me a strange look. *Great, Sophie. Now, not only are you an outsider, you're also crazy.*

I shook my head as I stepped into the classroom. I was about twenty minutes early and it was still empty.

I sat down at my desk determined to make some progress on the work I'd fallen behind on.

As I worked through the last of my math problems, I couldn't help but take a minute to check my phone. Still nothing.

"You really want me to text you, huh?" Wes grinned as he sat down in the desk beside mine.

Many of the other students had begun to filter into the classroom as well.

"No, it's not about you." I meant my words to be funny, but they came out harsh.

Why wasn't she calling me?

"Someone else?" He leaned across his desk and peered at my phone. "Did you find yourself someone else to insult?"

"Huh?" I glanced over at him, then frowned.

"Are you okay?" His eyes narrowed with concern.

"I'm fine." I looked back at my phone and fired off a quick text to my mother.

He stared at me for a moment, then turned back to the front of the classroom as the teacher stepped inside.

Mrs. Davis gave a reminder about the project being due the next day.

I looked over at Wes, but he had his nose buried in his tablet, probably playing another video game.

As I sank down in my chair, I thought about the reasons why my mother might not be calling. Was she hurt? Was she too wrapped up in Dale? Had Dale turned into a control freak that didn't let her use her phone? Maybe that was why he'd been so eager to send me away.

As class let out, I headed for the door while dialing my mom's number. As it went to voicemail yet again, I groaned and shoved my phone back into my pocket.

"Hey." Wes caught my arm as I turned in the opposite direction down the hallway. "Fi, what's going on? You seem upset. You know I was just joking around earlier, right?"

"Yes, I know." I looked at him as he stared at me. He might understand. Maby certainly wouldn't. She was used to spa days with her mother, not having to track her down for fear that something terrible had happened to her. "It's just family stuff."

"Okay." He steered me down a quieter hallway. "Tell me about it."

"It's not a big deal, I'm probably just overreacting." I shifted the strap of my backpack and looked past him toward the hallway I should have been walking down to get to my next class.

"Fi, are we friends or not?" He met my eyes. "I know you're far from home. I know you're still getting to know everyone here. But in case you haven't noticed, Maby adopted you and that means we've all adopted you."

"Oh?" I smiled. "I didn't realize that."

"It's true." He tipped his head toward mine. "So tell me."

SIXTEEN

Friends. Yes, friends.

That's what I told myself as I stared at Wes. What better way to show that I was his friend than to confide a little bit about my life?

"It's my mother." I leaned back against the wall and looked up at the ceiling. "I don't even know how to explain her. But she's gone silent on me and I'm not sure what that means."

"I don't hear from my dad unless I'm in trouble." Wes grinned. "Isn't silence a good sign?"

"Not in her case. She's always getting herself into some kind of predicament, and without me around to help her, I'm not sure she'll be able to find her way out of it." I looked over at him. "Silence from her usually means that things are bad and getting worse."

"I'm sorry." He frowned. "That must be pretty stressful—to feel like you have to take care of her."

"She's just so impulsive." I closed my eyes. "She chases down every idea she has and then wonders how she got lost."

"Sounds like she's pretty interesting."

"No." I opened my eyes and looked at him. "She's exhausting. I've never been able to keep up with her. When I was a kid, I got really good at math because I had to figure out how to make sure that the bills were paid. I can't tell you how many times we had the electricity or water cut off. It's not an easy way to live."

"I imagine it's not." He leaned back against the wall beside me. "It must be hard for you—to be surrounded by people who've never had to deal with things like that."

"We all have problems, they're just different." I glanced at him. "I'm sure she's fine. She always tells me I'm too paranoid."

"Well, I might have to agree with her there." He nudged my shoulder with his and smiled.

"Thanks." I laughed. "Glad we had this talk."

"I'm not saying she's not wrong about everything else. You shouldn't have had to be the parent, Fi—that's too much to ask of any kid. But I do think you could stand to loosen up a little and have some fun." He straightened up as the second bell chimed. "Look, I've already helped you to learn how to be late for class."

"Great." I winced and hurried down the hall. "Thanks for listening, Wes!" I waved to him over my shoulder, then ran full force to my next class.

My first week was not exactly going as planned. I did feel a little better, just telling Wes the truth. Now I wasn't the only one that knew my mother had gone silent and that it could lead to terrible things.

After the last class of the day, I sent Wes a quick text.

WE NEED to finish our project. Can we meet?

I WENT BACK to my dorm room, changed, and gathered my notebook and tablet. Then I checked my phone. No text from my mother. No text from Wes. Maybe he had things to finish up first.

I tried not to panic. The project had to be turned in the next day.

After an hour and still no response from Wes, I began to pace. At least I had caught up on the rest of my homework.

"I'll pin him down at dinner." I nodded to myself, then tried calling my mother again. This time it went straight to voicemail.

Unnerved, I decided I needed to get out of my own head and around other people. I found Maby in the living room.

"What are you up to?" I sat down beside her.

"Ugh, stupid math homework." She frowned as she pointed to the book in her lap. "Is this even English?"

"Well, it's numbers." I flashed a smile at her. "I could help you with it, if you'd like?"

"Really?" Her eyes widened. "Yes! Please! I will love you forever."

"Okay, sounds good." I laughed. As I began to explain the formula to her, I noticed that she had a hard time understanding it. I wondered how long she had been struggling in her classes. "Have you ever asked the teacher for more instruction?" I looked up at her.

"No way. I can't ruin my reputation like that." She frowned. "Besides, you can't help stupid, right?"

"Maby." I looked into her eyes. "You're not stupid. Not at all."

"Says you, but this math book says differently." She groaned. "I should just give up."

"No way. I'll help you get caught up. It's really not as hard as you think." I started to explain a few of the things I thought she needed refreshers on.

Soon she was smiling as she got each question right.

"Wow, I've never been able to understand how to do this before. Thank you so much." She hugged me.

"Of course. Anytime you need help just let me know."

Thrilled that I'd been able to help her after all that she'd done for me, my mood boosted. But the moment I looked at my phone and saw no text or call from either my mother or Wes, it crashed again.

In the cafeteria at dinner, I watched for Wes.

He had to be there, right? I'd seen him after class, we'd been friendly, why would he just bail on me now?

He wouldn't. I had to have faith in him.

That faith faded as I finished dinner and Wes still hadn't stepped into the cafeteria.

"Any idea where Wes is? We're supposed to finish our project today." I stood up from the table with the others.

"Aren't you his keeper now?" Apple smirked.

"Shh!" Candy huffed at her.

"I don't know where he is right now, but he missed his last two classes today." Mick shrugged. "It's just something that Wes does sometimes."

"Great." I was annoyed that he hadn't texted me, but I was also a little worried. Had something happened?

I waited an hour after dinner. When I still hadn't heard from him, I decided to take matters into my own hands. He could ignore me all he wanted, but I needed a good grade on the assignment.

I checked the common room and the game room and then I walked all through the courtyard. After that, I headed for the small library. I knew he'd taken girls there before. As much as I didn't want to interrupt him and a girl, I wasn't going to get a failing grade just so that he could have a little fun.

When I stepped into the library, I heard a faint commotion, then another door on the other side of the library close. I walked further into the library and spotted Wes at one of the long tables in the back of the room.

"Wes." I walked toward him as he quickly ran his fingers through his hair.

"Hey, Fi." He turned to look at me, a faint smile on his lips.

"You didn't text me back." I clenched my teeth. Was that lipstick on his cheek?

"I know, I just got busy." He cleared his throat. "We can finish it up now though, right? We still have time. I was just about to text you."

"Sure." I sat down at the table with him. Yes, that was lipstick on his cheek and on his neck.

My chest ached with anger, and though I hated to admit it, jealousy. Who was she? I guessed a cheerleader, someone much prettier than me, someone that he'd rather spend time with.

"Great." He flipped his notebook open. "Did you hear from your mom yet?"

"No, she hasn't texted me either." I snapped my notebook open.

"Alright, I'm sorry." He reached for my hand.

I pulled it back. "It's fine. You were busy." I did my best not to look at him.

"Things got a little hectic this afternoon. My dad showed up." He brushed his hair back from his eyes and sat back in his chair.

"Your dad?" I looked up at him. "Why? Were you in trouble for skipping your last two classes?"

"Spying on me again?" He grinned.

"More like I didn't want to fail my first major assignment. I know this is all a joke to you, but I can't risk not getting good grades while I'm here. It could make a huge difference in my life." I shook my head. "I don't expect you to understand that."

"I understand." He ran his hand across his forehead. "I wasn't going to let you fail."

"Why was your dad here?" I met his eyes.

"He needed to parade me around for one of his clients. Sometimes they want him to come to a family dinner and of course then I have to play my role as his son." He looked down at his notebook. "It doesn't matter, I got a nice steak out of it."

"It does matter." I put my hand over his, despite my better judgment. "I'm sorry that he treats you like that."

"It's alright." He picked up his pen. "Let's get this done."

SEVENTEEN

It took us almost two hours, but we managed to finish the assignment.

As I watched Wes pack up his things, I thought this might be the last time I would ever be alone with him. We'd had a project and now the project was complete. Maybe that was for the best, since my silly crush had really begun to interfere with my ability to think clearly.

"There. No failing, right?" He stood up from the table.

"Right." I nodded and stood up as well. "Sorry for interrupting earlier."

"Interrupting what?" He zipped his bag.

"Never mind. I'll see you in class tomorrow." I started toward the door.

"I'll walk you back. It's late." He caught up to me.

"You can't walk me back." I laughed as I looked back at him. "It's the girls' dormitory."

"Oh, right. No rule-breaking." He grinned. "Or maybe just this once? I need to talk to Maby about what we're doing on Saturday anyway."

"You're going?" I swallowed hard as he fell into step

beside me.

"Wouldn't miss it." He held the exterior door open for me and we both stepped out into the courtyard.

Although it was dark, there were plenty of lights that illuminated the area. We walked right past the statue I'd been pinned against earlier. My heart fluttered as I recognized it.

"I'm really looking forward to it—to Saturday."

"Good." He led me to the entrance of the girls' dormitory, then took a quick look around. "All clear." He pulled the door open. "Shall we?"

"This seems like a bad idea." I frowned as I glanced around as well.

"Don't worry, I'm slippery, remember?" He winked at me, then gave me a playful push through the door.

As we hurried up the stairs to the second floor, I couldn't help but be nervous. I didn't want to get in trouble, but I also didn't want rumors flying that I'd been seen sneaking around with Wes in the girls' dorm.

We were almost to my room, when a sharp whistle made me cringe.

Wes groaned and turned around to face Mrs. Reed.

"Just what are you two up to?" She crossed her arms as she looked between us.

"Mrs. Reed, this young woman was out after curfew." Wes crossed his arms and looked at me with wide eyes. "I had to make sure she got back to her room safe and sound."

"Is that so?" Mrs. Reed raised an eyebrow. "Sophie?"

"I'm sorry. I lost track of time." My heart pounded as I wondered if she might kick me out of the school right then and there.

"Get out of here, Wes." Mrs. Reed pointed down the hall. "Straight outside. I'll be calling Mr. Carver to make sure that you are in your room in five minutes. Understand?"

"Yes, ma'am." He nodded to her, cast a wink in my direction, then jogged back down the hallway.

"I'm really sorry, Mrs. Reed." I met her eyes as my hands trembled.

"You should be. Wes is nothing but trouble." She pointed her finger straight at me. "*You* could do much better. Now get into your room and get to bed. It's a school night."

"Yes, ma'am." I let myself into the dorm room and found Maby waiting on the other side of the door.

"Did you just get whistled by Mrs. Reed?" She clapped her hands gleefully.

"Maybe." I flopped down on the sofa.

"Were you out there with Wes?" She sat down next to me.

"He said he wanted to talk to you." I looked over at her. "About Saturday."

"Ah, I see." She pursed her lips. "Doubtful, since he's already texted me four times about it."

"Oh, *you* he texts." I rolled my eyes. "It doesn't matter. Our project is done, which means we're done." I yawned. "I need to get some sleep."

"Alright, have a good night." Maby stood up from the sofa. "Thanks so much for your help. I think I'm ready for my math test tomorrow."

"You're going to do great." I smiled at her, then stepped into my room.

Once I was sprawled out in bed, I grabbed my phone off the bedside table. I flipped through the texts I'd received from my mother in the past. No new texts. No calls.

"Where are you?" I frowned.

With my imagination running wild, I had a difficult time falling asleep.

I woke the next morning with my phone still in my hand, the alarm blaring. I turned it off and wiped at my eyes. It was the same cycle as usual. My mother would disappear, get herself into something ridiculous, I would worry about her and find a way to bail her out. Even though I was at Oak Brook and making real friends for the first time in my life, I still felt as if I was stuck back in her life with her.

"No." I set the phone down and headed for the shower. "Not this time. If she's gotten herself into some kind of mess, she can find her own way out of it."

As the hot water rushed over me, I imagined it washing away the past seventeen years. I didn't have to be that Sophie anymore. I could be Fi. I could be someone who smiled and laughed and bent the rules now and then. I could be someone with a future and so much to look forward to.

When I settled at the table with Maby for breakfast, she smiled at me.

"That's new."

"What's new?" I looked across the table at her.

"You smiling in the morning. I don't know, you just look happier." She shrugged.

"I feel happier." I smiled, then dug into my cereal.

As I ate, Maby described our upcoming outing to me—practically minute by minute. I didn't mind that she wanted to organize everything. It felt amazing that she'd gone to so much trouble just for me. I had a real friend and that made me feel like the luckiest person in the world.

As I stepped into my first class of the day with my poem ready to be turned in, I felt another burst of confidence. Wes had helped me dig deeper into every line, until I felt as if I'd created something special.

I settled in my desk at the back of the class and soaked in my surroundings. I was really here, in one of the best schools in the country, a place I'd never imagined I could be. It wasn't a mistake or a joke. It was real.

Wes sat down in the desk next to mine and glanced over with a smile.

I smiled in return. And that was all it was. A smile.

Maybe there was still a part of me that tingled at the sight of him, but it was more important to me that he remained my friend. I'd never been part of a group before and now I couldn't imagine my life without them in it.

I handed my poem to the teacher, confident that she would find it at the very least acceptable.

Wes leaned close to me. "Can I confess something?"

"Sure." I met his eyes.

"I've never looked forward to turning something in before. Thanks for working with me."

"No problem." I smiled. "You are quite talented, you know."

"Talented?" He squinted at me. "I don't recall that being in that first poem you wrote."

"Okay, I might have left a few things out." I laughed.

"Sophie! Wes!" Mrs. Davis called out. "Enough with the chatter."

I blushed and looked down at my desk. He did always manage to get me into trouble. But maybe that wasn't such a bad thing.

The next day blew by as I got caught up in everyone's excitement about the weekend. I finally felt more comfortable in all of my classes. I'd met a few more people and I didn't feel like I was so much of an outsider.

Maybe that would change, but for the moment, I felt welcome and not so strange.

That night my body buzzed with excitement for the trip the next day. I couldn't wait to be in the middle of the city, exploring a place I'd always dreamed of visiting.

This was my life now and I was determined to enjoy it.

EIGHTEEN

"Today is the day!" Maby hollered.

I blinked, then fully opened my eyes to the sound of banging on my bedroom door.

"Okay!" I laughed and stumbled out of bed. The blanket caught around my feet and I had to catch myself on my desk. "Maby, you're going to wake the whole dorm!"

"Too bad. They can't come." She laughed.

I pulled open the door and found her already dressed. "Wow, you were serious about leaving early, weren't you?"

"Yes! You're not even dressed? Get moving! I've already made us some bagels to take with us." She suddenly grabbed my arm. "Oh, wait! I forgot. Wes and Mick gave me this for you." She grinned as she held out a box to me.

"What is it?" I raised an eyebrow.

"Don't know, you're going to have to open it."

I sat down on the edge of my bed and opened the lid.

"Oh no, you have to be kidding me! I am not wearing this!" I laughed and shook my head at the same time.

"Don't be like that! The guys had it made just for you! Isn't that sweet?" Maby laughed as well. She snatched the t-shirt out of the box and held it up for me to see.

"I can't possibly wear that in public. No way!" I stared at the bold black letters that spelled out four words. *New York City Virgin*. What were they thinking?

"I think it's great." She tossed it at me. "Just try it on. I'll snap a picture of you in it and that should be enough for them."

"Fine." I groaned as I stepped into my bathroom to change. Even though I was horrified by the gift, I did actually think it was sweet of them to have it made for me. There was no chance the old Sophie would wear this shirt. No chance at all.

I pulled it over my head, then looked in the mirror.

I wasn't Sophie anymore. I was Fi. Would Fi wear it?

I stepped back into my room and posed for Maby's picture.

"It fits great." She giggled.

"You know, it does." I smoothed the material down over my stomach. "It fits so well that I think I should just go ahead and wear it."

"Seriously?" Her eyes widened. "Are you really going to?"

"Why not?" I grinned. "It's time I had some fun, right?"

"Yes, it is!" She squealed, then hugged me. "I knew you would be so much fun once you loosened up."

"Thanks?" I laughed.

"Oh, you know what I mean!" She waved her hand at me. "Let's go, we have to hurry. I have a cab waiting for us. We need to get to Battery Park before the crowds."

I let her sweep me along, but by the time we boarded the double-decker boat, my heart was heavier. I still hadn't heard a word from my mother. It was Saturday. What possible excuse could she have?

I followed my friends up to the top deck and joined in their laughter. But for just a moment I closed my eyes and wished as hard as I could. *Please, Mom, please, just this once, don't blow this for us.*

When I opened my eyes again, the beauty of New York City sprawled out before me. I watched the skyline of the buildings glide by as the boat moved further out into the water. The sight of it stirred so many ideas within me. There were so many places I wanted to see.

Then there she was, torch erect and looking regal as ever against the pale blue sky. My eyes stung with tears. I hadn't expected to feel so emotional.

"You okay?" Wes draped his arm around me. "Getting a little seasick?"

"No." I took a deep breath. "I'm just amazed."

"Amazed?" He smiled as he looked at me.

"I've seen pictures, but I never thought I'd be here in person." I ducked my head as I wiped at my eyes. "Don't tease me."

"I won't." He tightened his grasp on my shoulders. "Not even a little bit."

As we clambered off the boat and toward the base of the statue, Maby held up her hands to stop us.

"Alright, now slow down, everyone! I want to make sure we stick together! I've outlined several points of interest that we need to see. Please don't skip ahead!"

Candy tilted her head to the side as she looked at Maby. "No way, hon, you're being way too serious." She looked over at Apple and Mick. "Race you to the crown!" She squealed as she took off for the entrance.

"Wait! Stop!" Maby ran after them.

"Oh, this is not going well." I laughed and then cringed.

"Don't worry, Maby tries to do this every time we do something and it never works. Stick with me, I'll show you around." Wes smiled.

"Thanks." I followed him through the entrance, where Maby found us again.

"At least you two have some sense. Now for the tour." She walked me through each exhibit.

Wes lingered by my side but remained mostly silent. I wondered if he'd have been happier with the others, but he didn't complain. Maybe he wanted to see the reactions to my t-shirt. To my surprise, there weren't many. I guessed that in New York City there wasn't much that people hadn't seen.

Finally, Maby led us to the crown, where Candy, Mick, and Apple lounged on the floor with their phones.

"It's about time." Candy rolled her eyes.

"I can't believe you do this every time!" Maby put her hands on her hips. "Would it kill you to follow directions?"

"Probably." Candy flashed her a smile.

"Look at this." Wes led me to one of the openings in the crown. "This, I still find amazing." He stood close to me as I looked through the window.

"Wow!" I breathed the word as I took in the sight before me. "It feels like I can see forever."

"If you come this way, you can see more of the city." He led me to another window while Maby and Candy continued to argue.

"Are they okay?" I frowned as I glanced over at them.

"They're fine. Trust me, I'd be more worried if they weren't arguing." He grinned.

"That's it, I'm done. I'm going to find some decent coffee!" Maby huffed. "Who's with me?"

"I'm dying for a coffee." Mick nodded.

"I could go for some hot chocolate." Apple jumped to her feet.

"Coffee. Now that sounds like a good plan." Candy winked

at her. "Let me guess, you've researched the best coffee joints nearby?"

"So what if I did? That's just proper planning!" Maby placed her hands on her hips.

"You guys go ahead." Wes grabbed my hand. "Fi and I will catch up with you."

"See, you ruined everything." Maby rolled her eyes at Candy as she started for the spiral stairs.

"Me?" Candy followed right behind her. "How is this my fault?"

"Nothing is ruined, it was great, Maby!" I called out to her, though I doubted she could hear me over the arguing. Wes's hand around mine had me distracted and I had no idea why he'd told them to leave without us. "Shouldn't we go with them?"

"Let them go." He tugged me a little closer to him. "I grew up around here. I know a special place to take you."

"Don't you think they should come with us?" I watched as Maby and Candy continued to squabble.

"Not this time. This time, I just want to show you." He looked into my eyes. "Okay?"

"Okay." I felt my heart skip a beat.

No, it wasn't okay. It wasn't okay, because when I looked at him, I didn't want to just be alone with him. I wanted so much more. It wasn't okay because the rule was at least three people together. It wasn't okay because his hand wrapped around mine left me dizzy and confused.

But it didn't matter. There was no way I was going to turn him down.

NINETEEN

When we reached Battery Park, Wes led me off the boat with his hand wrapped around mine.

"Don't worry, it's not far."

I felt drawn in by the excitement in his voice. Where was he taking me that was so important? And why?

The "why" made me shiver with anticipation. He'd separated me from the others. He was sharing something with just me. Didn't that mean something?

He looked back at me and smiled—not the all-knowing smile that always got under my skin, but a warm and relaxed smile that I'd never seen before.

I smiled back as my mind raced.

Please, Sophie. Just don't let your imagination run wild.

When we finally stopped, he turned to face me. "Fi." He met my eyes. "Do you trust me?"

"I barely know you." I crossed my arms as I studied him.

"Fair point." He licked his lips. "Do you trust me enough to let me surprise you?"

"What exactly do you want me to do?" I took a slight step back. "I don't want to be arrested."

"You won't be." He moved closer. "I won't let anything bad happen, I promise. But this will be so much better if you let me do one thing."

"What thing?" I eyed him with some concern. The glimmer in his eyes was new.

"Blindfold you." He slid his hand into his pocket and pulled out the tie from his school uniform.

Had he planned this? My body tensed. What exactly had he planned?

"I don't think so." I shook my head.

"It'll just be for a minute." He held the tie out to me. "You can do it yourself."

"This is silly, Wes. Why don't you just tell me what we're doing?" I stared at the tie but didn't take it.

"I could, but it wouldn't be the same." He frowned. "Can't you just trust me a little bit?"

"Why should I?" I raised an eyebrow.

"I got you an A, right?" He smiled.

"Fine." I took the tie from him. "But just remember, I'm not one of those girls that wants to disappear somewhere with you, okay?"

"Okay?" He laughed. "And for the record, I know you're not one of those girls."

His words stung, even though I wasn't sure what I wanted to hear. Did that mean he could never think of me that way? Was he laughing because it was so absurd for me to even imagine that he might be the least bit interested?

Embarrassed, I tried to wrap the tie around my eyes. My hands trembled as I tried to tie the knot.

"Here."

Startled by how close the sound of his voice was, I jerked to the side.

"Relax, Fi." He sighed and rested his hands on my shoulders.

I felt the weight and warmth of them and I did relax, despite all the reasons I thought that I shouldn't. I felt his fingers as they trailed through my hair pulling it gently back over my shoulders. I felt his fingertips as they brushed against the back of my head while he tied the blindfold.

"That's not too tight, is it?"

"No." The word came out as a whisper.

"Don't worry, you don't have to wear it long." He spoke just as softly.

I felt him take my hand, then lead me forward. I heard the turn of a lock then became aware that we were walking through a door. I heard something whir to life and I could detect a faint flicker through the blindfold. Music began to play. It was classical and whimsical. Piano notes danced all around me.

"Wes? Where are we?" I tightened my grasp on his hand.

"Promise not to laugh?" His voice drifted just beside my ear.

I shivered, not from cold or fear, but from curiosity and anticipation. "I promise."

"Okay." He tugged the knot in the tie free and I felt its silky surface drift across my face as I opened my eyes.

Immediately I saw giant glass fish bathed in glowing light that shifted and twisted in time with the music. My mind didn't know how to make sense of it, but my heart swelled with its beauty.

"This place is amazing." I turned slowly and looked up at the lights that painted the ceiling and walls.

"It's a carousel. My mom used to bring me here when I was little." He trailed his fingertips along the curved glass of one of the fish. "For a little while, I thought I had imagined it, until I found this place again." He met my eyes. "I managed to convince the owner—with a lot of charm and a lot of cash—to give me a key."

"It must have been so hard to lose her." I turned my attention back to him. The faint bluish glow outlined his features in a strange, dream-like way.

"It was." He met my eyes, then looked away quickly. "Everyone says to me that it must have been so hard, but it's not like it really got any easier. I come here sometimes—not as much as I used to—but just to try to get everything to calm down in my head." He closed his eyes. "But it doesn't always work."

I stared at him in the semi-darkness. In that moment he didn't look so cool, so untouchable. My arms ached with the urge to hug him, but I ignored the instinct.

Friends, I reminded myself. No need to send any mixed messages.

"Is it working now?" I watched as he eased himself down onto a ledge at the edge of the carousel.

"A little." He looked up at me and smiled.

"Thank you for bringing me here." I sat down beside him, so close that our knees brushed in the process.

As I started to shift away, I felt him lean closer.

My heart fluttered. I closed my eyes and tried to force myself to ignore the sensations that rippled through my body.

"I thought with everything going on with your mom, you might need a place like this." He frowned. "I know you're worried about her."

"You're right. I am worried about her." I took a deep breath and looked through the colored glass. The way it warped and colored everything beyond it made me feel as if the world had transformed around me. "I'm sorry. When I complain about my mom, it probably sounds terrible to you."

"No, it doesn't." He rested his hand against mine, our pinkies touching. "Not every mother is the same. To be honest, I don't know if my mother was a good mother. I don't remember. But I do know that she wanted to be around me, which is a lot more than I can say for my dad these days."

"Mine too." I smiled some. "He walked out and I never saw him again. Then again, who knows if he even was my father? My mom isn't known for telling the truth." My chest tightened at the thought of her. I turned away as tears threatened my eyes.

"Fi, it's okay to still love her." He wrapped his hand around mine. "She may never be the kind of mother you deserve, but she's still your mother."

"Yes, she is." I drew a deep breath. "I just hope that she isn't in some kind of trouble." I pulled my hand gently from his. "We should get back."

"Right, okay." He ran his hand along his knee and frowned. "If that's what you want."

"I think I've taken up enough of your time." I shrugged as I walked around the glass fish. "I'm sure you have other things to do."

"Other things to do?" He stood up and walked towards me. "What makes you think that?"

"You're in demand." I flashed him a smile.

"Am I?" He paused beside me and stared at me. "You want to leave without a ride?" He gestured to a nearby fish.

"We can't turn it on, can we?" I smiled a little. "Carousels have always been my favorite."

"All I have to do is flip a switch." He tipped his head toward the nearby control panel. "But if you don't want to stay..."

"I do." I smiled.

"Pick one out." He grinned as he walked over to the control panel.

I looked at all the fish seats. Each one was just as beautiful as the next, but they were all different shapes and designs.

I found one that was mostly open. I was about to climb into

it, when Wes reached my side again. The ride jerked to life and we both stumbled forward.

As I felt myself lose my balance, Wes's arm wrapped around my waist in the same moment that he fell. He landed in the seat I'd chosen and he pulled me down into his lap with him.

"Hold on." He laughed as the fish continued to glide forward.

TWENTY

My heart raced as I felt my body press against his. How had this happened?

Seconds ago, I could barely handle our hands touching and now I was practically lying on top of him. Could he feel my heart pounding? I wasn't sure how he couldn't.

"Look, Fi." He pushed some of my hair out of his face and pointed up at the ceiling. "Doesn't it look like water?"

"Yes." I breathed the word, unable to speak any louder. The shifting colors on the ceiling did allow me to relax a little. I noticed that his hand lingered on my shoulder, not far from my cheek. His other arm draped lazily across my stomach. I could feel the tickle of his breath along the curve of my neck.

He'd confided something in me, he'd shared a special place with me, and all I could focus on was his skin against mine, the brush of his chin against my hair as he shifted his head, the way his arm tightened just a little around me when the fish spun.

Please, Sophie. I closed my eyes tight. Please, don't let yourself get carried away.

As the ride came to a stop, I felt him shift under me, but his arm remained around me.

"Did you like it?" He sat forward some, so that his lips hovered not far from my ear.

I nodded, unable to speak as my mind spun with the effects of his warmth wrapped around me.

"Sophie?" He pulled some hair away from my face and sat up straighter.

I suddenly became aware that he was likely waiting for me to get up. I twisted in his grasp in an attempt to get to my feet, but my foot slid on the edge of the fish and I only succeeded in falling back toward him—only this time, we were face-to-face.

"Easy." He caught me as he smiled and looked up into my eyes. "You don't have to hurry."

With our lips inches apart, I felt that odd rush that I'd had on the first day that I'd looked into his eyes. It was more than just excitement. It wasn't quite desperation. It was a deep need, like a thirst that I would do anything to quench.

I felt frozen by the moment, as if all time had stopped and I had no idea how to get it moving again.

Then his fingertips caressed the curve of my cheek and my heart jolted back to life in a frenzy of beats. He lifted his head and his lips neared mine. I watched the journey in slow motion, knowing that with each millisecond that passed they came closer.

Just before our lips might have collided, I turned my head to the side.

It was just a fantasy. He wasn't trying to kiss me, he was trying to get up and I was in his way.

With my mind focused on this, I pulled away from him and stood up. "Thanks, Wes, that was a lot of fun." I looked at the ceiling instead of him.

He was silent as he got to his feet.

I looked over at him and noticed how tight his lips were and the way his jaw tensed.

Had I upset him by being so ridiculous? Could he tell what I'd been thinking?

"You're right, we should go." He walked over to the control panel and turned the switch off.

The ride stopped—so did the lights and the music. The room was illuminated only by the pale light that poured in through the windows and the exit signs.

"It's getting late." He cleared his throat.

"Right." I forced a smile. "I'll bet Maby loves this place too."

"She doesn't know about it." He walked toward me, his eyes narrowed. "I don't want anyone else to know about it. Okay?"

"Sure." My breath caught in my throat. He had taken me somewhere that no one else knew about? But why? "I won't tell anyone."

"I know what you must think of me." He slid his hands into his pockets as he stared at me.

"What do you mean?" I watched him for any sign of what he might be thinking.

"In the library the other night..." He ran his hand along his cheek where the lipstick had been. "I didn't know that she'd left anything behind."

"It's okay, it's not my business really." I looked down at my feet.

"That's not who I really am, Fi." He murmured his words. "I know you have no reason to believe that, but it's the truth."

"You don't have to explain yourself to me." I took his hand, though my heart fluttered as I did. "I'm your friend. I'm not here to judge you."

He looked up at the ceiling, then took a slow breath.

"I just want you to know. Sometimes—sometimes, I get so messed up in the head, I just need a way to stop thinking about everything. There's always someone else available that wants to stop thinking too." He met my eyes again. "I don't know why I do it."

"Maybe..." I searched his eyes as I tightened my grasp on his hand. "Maybe you just don't want to feel so alone, and having someone in your arms—well, I'd imagine it makes it better."

"But it never lasts." He swallowed hard. "I mean, it's only kissing. I don't want you to think it's more than that." He looked away from me. "Most of the time, I just feel worse after I spend time with a girl—like none of it really matters."

"Wes." I released his hand and touched his cheek. As I turned his face back to mine, I could barely breathe. It didn't matter in that moment that I had a silly crush or that he would never feel the same way about me. All that mattered was that he was in pain and I wanted him to know that he wasn't alone. "Disappearing doesn't fix anything. Trust me, I know. Even if you can forget everything for a little while, it's always there. It never goes away. No matter what you think, you don't have to be alone. You have me."

"I do?" He reached up and grasped my wrists.

"Yes, of course. And Maby and Apple and Mick and Candy." I drew my hands away. "We're always going to be here for you."

"Thanks." He took a deep breath and offered a small smile. "That means a lot. It's good to hear."

"Well, I mean it. Maybe next time you start to feel that way, you could just find me. We could talk about it." I smiled. "I can be a good listener."

"Yes, you can be." He started toward the door. "I'd better get you back before Maby sends out a search party." He pulled the door open which allowed light to spill in.

In the stark sunlight he looked like Wes again, with that infuriating smile. But now I knew something about him. I knew that when he pulled a girl into his arms, it wasn't just about pleasure. It was about escape. He was on the run—not unlike I was—from the pain inside him.

"You coming?"

"Sure." I joined him at the door, then stepped through it.

His hand settled on the small of my back as he guided me down the sidewalk. It lingered there as he hailed a cab.

When he pulled open the door for me, I slid inside, remembering the sensation of being so close to him. As he slid inside beside me, I wondered if I had imagined his lips getting so close to mine.

The engine revved and the cab bolted off into the traffic, which caused me to rock and slip a little against the vinyl seat. He caught my hand and held it. He didn't let go the entire ride.

As the cab pulled up to the school, I glanced over at him.

He met my eyes, then released my hand. "Better hurry and get back to your dorm. I wouldn't want to get you in trouble." He winked at me, then stepped out of the cab.

TWENTY-ONE

On my way back to my room, I couldn't shake the memory of his hand closing over mine. He didn't have to hold it the whole way home. Maybe I wasn't imagining how close his lips had come. What if he really did feel the same kind of connection to me that I did to him?

I gave myself permission to believe it, just for a moment. I couldn't resist the smile that spread across my face.

Wes and me? The thought made my toes wiggle in my shoes. I'd never felt this way about anyone before. Certainly, Wes wasn't the type of boy that I expected to feel this way about. But maybe there was something to what my mother always said—love is love, baby, and you can't fight that. Of course, *she* said that about every guy she'd ever dated. I cringed at that thought and the reminder that I still hadn't heard from her.

I stepped into my dorm room and found Maby on the sofa waiting for me.

"Where were you?"

I was so distracted by the fantasy of Wes and me having a

happily-ever-after that the edge to her tone didn't bother me much.

"With Wes." I flopped down on the sofa beside her.

"Yes, I know you were with Wes." She pursed her lips. "Where?"

"I can't tell you that." I closed my eyes as I remembered the first moment I'd seen the place. "It was just a place that he wanted me to see."

"Did it have something to do with this?" Maby cleared her throat.

I opened my eyes and saw that she was dangling a piece of paper in front of my face. A piece of paper covered in Wes's distinct handwriting.

"Maby!" I snatched the poem from her hand. "Did you go in my room and take this?"

"I went in your room to see if you had a book I needed for my weekend homework. I found it on the floor right next to your bed." She sighed as she sat back against the sofa. "I know that's Wes's handwriting."

"So." I folded the paper up as my mind spun. "It doesn't mean anything. It was just part of the assignment we were working on."

"Sure." She quirked an eyebrow. "I know Wes and I know that he doesn't write like that. He doesn't say things like that either." She shook her head. "I knew it was a bad idea for you two to be alone together."

"It's not a big deal. We're just friends." I forced down a faint bolt of excitement over what she said. He didn't write or say things like that? Did that mean he might have meant what he said?

"Fi." Maby took my hands and looked into my eyes. "I really like Wes, I've told you this. I think he's a great guy, and I hope that one day he will find someone that he can spend the rest of his life with. But that day is not today, that day is years from now. Wes doesn't stay with just one girl. Do you hear me?"

"Maybe you don't know him as well as you think." I drew my hands away. "People can change."

"You're right, they can, but not overnight. I do know him, better than I'd like to. Did you know that he used to date Candy?" She met my eyes. "I'm telling you the truth."

"Okay." I shrugged. "They're still friends, so it couldn't have been that bad."

"It *was* bad. It took me weeks to get her straightened out. After that I made him promise me that he wouldn't try anything with our group of friends. I guess he isn't standing by that promise anymore." She stood up from the sofa and narrowed her eyes. "I can't believe he's doing this."

"Wait, stop!" I stood up and caught her by the shoulders. "Listen, I know you're just trying to protect me—I know you're just being a good friend—but you have to trust me when I tell you that he's not *doing* anything. There were moments today when he could have, but he didn't, because he's not interested in me like that. We're friends, that's all. That's all we'll ever be."

My heart sank as I heard my own words. It was good that I forced myself to admit it.

"I don't know, I've seen the way he looks at you." She shook her head.

"It's nothing." I took a deep breath. "Wes isn't breaking any promises."

"Good." She met my eyes. "Because there's a dance next Friday night and you're going. Maybe you'll meet a boy."

"A dance?" I laughed. "I've never been to a dance in my life. There's no chance of that."

"Oh, you're going." She smiled. "Apple, Candy and I are going to take you shopping tomorrow."

"I'm not sure that's a good idea." I started to back away toward my room.

"You don't have a choice in the matter. It's time you stepped out a little bit." She raised an eyebrow. "I can't wait to get my hands on that hair."

"That sounds awful." I laughed as I batted her hand away from my hair. "I'm just not into that kind of stuff."

"No, the old you isn't into that kind of stuff." She placed her hands on her hips. "Don't you owe it to yourself to try it just once, just to see if you might enjoy it?"

"I guess." I sighed and rolled my eyes. "I suppose it couldn't hurt."

"It might hurt a little." She squinted at my hair. "You do have some tangles."

"Great." I laughed. "I'm beat. I'm going to go lie down for a bit." I waved her away from my hair. "Did you find the book you needed?"

"Uh—it turns out I didn't need it." She smiled. "In fact, I'd better get back to work on my assignment." She headed for her room.

As I stepped into my room, I guessed from her reaction that she hadn't been looking for a book. Had she been so worried about me being alone with Wes that she looked through my things? And what about Wes and Candy? If he'd broken her heart, would a promise to Maby be enough to stop him from doing the same to me?

I sat down on the edge of my bed and closed my eyes. It was easy to remember the near-kiss and his arm draped around me. It was much harder to hear him confess that he used girls as an escape. Even if they knew that it didn't mean anything to him, it still didn't feel right to me.

Did he want me to be his next escape? I pushed the thought out of my mind. All of it was just too confusing.

I picked up my phone and checked for a message from my mother.

Again nothing.

"What is going on, Mom? I'm not waiting around anymore to find out." I scanned through my contact list and found Dale's number. I had no idea if he would answer the phone, but I had to try.

As the phone rang, I braced myself. Would he be annoyed that I'd reached out to him?

"Hello?"

"Dale, it's Fi—" I shook my head. "I mean, Sophie. Angie's daughter."

"Sophie. Hi." He sounded flustered.

"I'm sorry to bother you, but I haven't been able to reach my mom. I'm sure you two are just busy having fun, but I just wanted to make sure everything was okay." I paused.

He was silent.

"Dale? *Is* everything okay?"

"Sophie, I'm sorry. I think you need to speak to your mother about that. I'll tell her to call you." He hung up the phone.

I stared at the phone in my hand.

What was that? Why hadn't he just put her on the phone? Why hadn't he answered when I asked if everything was okay?

My chest tightened as dread filled it. Something was definitely wrong.

TWENTY-TWO

The call with Dale left me so stunned that I barely noticed when Wes sat down beside me at dinner. I couldn't keep up with the conversation among my friends. I clutched my phone in my hand and waited, hoping for it to ring or buzz with a text. What could have happened that my mother's husband didn't want to tell me? Why was it so difficult for her to call me and tell me what was going on?

A horrible thought occurred to me. What if she was in jail? I'd had to bail her out once before—with the help of a drunken neighbor—but most of the time she didn't take things that far.

I closed my eyes and tried to force the thought to disappear.

"Fi, aren't you going to eat?" Wes nudged my tray toward me.

"Uh—no." I glanced at him and noticed for the first time how close he was to me. "I'm not feeling well."

"Delayed seasickness." Candy pointed her fork at me. "I've seen it before. Eat nothing but crackers or you will regret it."

"Maybe." I nodded.

I looked down at my plate. The food blurred together.

"She's just nervous because I told her about the dance." Maby smiled. "And she agreed to go."

"You did?" Wes grinned as he looked over at me.

"She didn't leave me much choice." I shrugged.

"Yes!" Apple clapped her hands enthusiastically. "I will take you to my favorite dress shop. The designer isn't very well known, but she's brilliant!"

"Uh..." I poked my fork into my food. "We might need to be on a smaller budget."

"Don't worry, you don't have to pay upfront. Your stepdad can send a check." Apple smiled. "You'll love it, trust me."

Stepdad.

I closed my eyes as my mind swirled again.

"Fi, are you okay?" Wes leaned closer to me.

"Actually, I think Candy is right. I'm just going to go lie down." I stood up from the table and carried my tray to the trash. I felt a wave of guilt as I scraped the untouched food into the garbage. How many nights had I wished to have more to eat? I set the tray on the counter, then headed out of the cafeteria.

With my mother's fate pressing on my mind, I didn't notice anyone behind me until I jumped when I felt a hand on my back. I spun around.

"Wes!" I met his eyes.

"Sorry, I didn't mean to scare you." He took a step back. "I just wanted to make sure that you were okay."

I was tempted to tell him everything—about the conversation with my mom's husband, about my concerns for her—but Maby's warning flashed through my mind.

"I just need to go lie down, that's all. It was such a great day." I smiled some. "Thanks to Maby—and to all you guys. I think I'm just a little worn out."

"You know you can tell me anything, right?" He shifted closer to me.

"Thanks, Wes." I nodded, then continued toward my room. His kindness reminded me that he did want to be my friend, and although that meant a lot to me, it also reminded me that he didn't want to be anything more.

I sprawled out on my bed and tried not to think about anything but the lights that had floated across the ceiling.

At some point I drifted off to sleep.

The next morning, I woke to the sound of laughter outside my door. Dazed and half-awake I walked toward it.

"Hello?" I opened the door and peeked out.

"Oh, sorry!" Apple clasped her hand over her mouth. "I didn't mean to wake you up."

"It's alright." I smiled at her and Candy, who was perched on the sofa beside her.

"It's about time you got up." Maby grinned as she handed me a bowl of cereal. "Eat fast, we have a lot of ground to cover today."

"Are you feeling better?" Candy frowned as she looked at me.

I thought about Maby's confession that Candy had once dated Wes. Knowing that made me wonder if it would bother Candy that I was interested in him. It was pointless to pretend that I wasn't at this point. Not that it really mattered.

"I'm feeling better, thanks." I carried the cereal bowl over to the table and sat down. "Are you sure you want to do this? I really don't need to go to the dance."

"You really do." Maby sat down at the table with me. "It's going to be great, trust me. There's even going to be a live band, and something outrageous always happens."

"Happens?" Candy grinned. "Don't you mean someone always orchestrates it?"

"Yes, okay, but it's still fun." Maby smiled. "Let us do this for you, Fi. It'll be fun, I promise."

"Pedicures!" Apple stuck her feet out and wiggled her toes.

"What?" I laughed. "I've never had one of those. Isn't it weird to let people touch your feet?"

"Not if you're paying them to do it." Candy grinned. "It's nice and relaxing. It's a little weird at first, I guess."

"I wouldn't know, I've been getting my nails done with my mom since I was still in diapers." Maby grinned. "And to me, it's always fun."

"I guess I could try it." I looked down at my bare toes. "Though I might scare them off."

"Trust me, they've seen worse." Candy winked at me.

Once we were in the cab, there was no turning back. I was surrounded by friends. It was something I had never experienced before. But the closer we got to our first destination, the more tense I felt. I didn't have any money to buy a dress. How could I explain that to them? They had probably always had the money to buy anything they wanted.

"You know, one of my favorite things to do is go to a thrift store and hunt for awesome vintage stuff." I lied a little. I did shop at thrift stores, but without any particular style in mind. I just bought whatever I could afford.

"Oh yeah, I've had some friends that like to do that." Apple scrunched up her nose. "But I mean, they're still clothes that were worn by someone else. That's the part I don't like."

"I've found some cool stuff hitting yard sales with my grandma." Candy smiled. "She has a good eye for fashion."

"Yard sales?" My eyes widened as I looked at her. "You go to yard sales?"

"Sure." She shrugged. "Why not? Usually we pay much more than what they're asking. My grandma calls them our random acts of kindness. It's kind of fun. Like a treasure hunt."

"I'd be willing to do a thrift store crawl with you one day." Maby met my eyes. "But not today. Today we are going to find you a brand new dress and have it tailored to suit your figure."

"Tailored?" I shook my head. "That seems like a lot."

Maby looked straight into my eyes and smiled. "Everything has already been taken care of. This is my treat."

"What?" My eyes widened.

"It's time you had a little princess treatment." She patted my knee. "You deserve it."

"It's too much, Maby." I shook my head. "Really, I can't accept it."

"Oh, you can and you will." She laughed. "Girls, tell her."

"Yeah, you don't want to say no to Maby. She'll make you regret it, and when I say regret it, I mean 'crawl on the floor sobbing your eyes out begging for her forgiveness' regret it." Apple winced. "Don't ask me how I know that."

"Apple, would I do something like that?" Maby offered a sweet smile.

"Yup." Candy shuddered. "Just go with it, Fi, trust me."

I couldn't help but laugh at the horrified look on Candy's face. "Thank you, Maby."

"You're welcome." She pointed to the store the cab had stopped in front of and lowered her voice. "But don't expect me not to have some input on what dress you go home with."

"Okay." I smiled nervously as I followed the others out of the cab. It was strange for me to be given so much, and although it made me a little uneasy, I promised myself I would do my best to enjoy it.

After hearing Dale's voice on the phone, I doubted that it would last much longer. I paused outside the door and sent a quick text to my mother.

WHERE ARE YOU? What did you do? Are you alright?

. . .

I TUCKED my phone back into my pocket and let my friends lead me into a world of white plush sofas and floor-to-ceiling mirrors. The dresses on display were far different than anything I'd ever seen in a thrift store.

As I watched Maby survey one in particular, my stomach flipped. Would she expect me to wear something as fancy as that?

Soon I was surrounded by three girls with three different dresses—each with an eager smile.

"Okay." I took a deep breath. "I guess this means I'm going to have to shave my legs?"

The horrified look in their eyes told me everything I needed to know.

I was definitely entering uncharted territory.

TWENTY-THREE

"Try this one first." Apple held out a royal blue dress with a long pleated skirt and a tiny low-cut top.

"I'm not sure that's something I could wear." I tipped my head to the side as I looked at it.

"No, silly—well, it certainly won't meet the dress code for the dance. But you don't have to just try on what you're going to buy. It's good to try on different styles just to see what you like and what looks good on you. So try it!"

"Okay, okay." I laughed and took all three dresses into the dressing room with me.

As I looked at the silky material and unique designs, I tried not to be overwhelmed. I was alone in a dressing room with three dresses that cost more than my entire wardrobe by far.

"Are you ready yet?" Candy called out.

I glanced toward the door. I hadn't even taken a dress off a hanger yet. "Almost." I hurried to change out of my clothes, then took down the blue dress. As I pulled it on, I braced myself for what I would see in the mirror. A dress wouldn't suddenly make me beautiful, that was for sure.

I squeezed my eyes shut, then forced myself to face the mirror. As I gazed at my own reflection, I was surprised at the way it hugged my frame. Where I didn't have curves before, I now saw some. No, it wasn't a miraculous transformation, but just the fit of the dress was enough to make a difference.

"Let's go!" Apple called out. "I can't wait to see!"

"Alright, alright." I laughed as I opened the door. I stood there in my worn-out socks and the most expensive dress I'd ever been near—let alone worn—and listened as my friends fawned over me. It wasn't exactly my favorite activity, but the warmth of their friendship left butterflies in my stomach.

This was real. I was finally part of a circle of friends.

"Try mine on next." Candy insisted. "You need something short to show off those legs." She cleared her throat. "I mean, once they're cleaned up a bit." She giggled.

"You know, women really should be allowed to have hairy legs if they want." Apple shrugged. "My mom doesn't shave hers."

"That's because your mom is a hippie." Maby quirked an eyebrow.

"And?" Apple smiled. "She's a happy hippie, isn't she?"

I grinned as I stepped back into the dressing room.

For the next few hours I tried on several different dresses. By the time I pulled the last one on, I was exhausted. The silver material clung to my frame as it edged down along my skin. The neckline was low, but not scandalously so. The skirt flared out just past my thighs and cut off a little below my knee.

When I turned to look at myself in the mirror, I didn't expect much. What I saw, however, took my breath away. I couldn't remember a single time in my life that I had looked in the mirror and been pleased by what I saw there. I wasn't just pleased, I was blown away. In fact, I wondered for a moment if I was hallucinating due to the endless changing of clothes. But there I was, with a figure—an actual figure. The color seemed to brighten my hair and my eyes.

"I promise, it's the last one." Maby spoke from just outside the door. "Let's see it."

"Okay." I took a deep breath. Would the others feel the same way about the dress? I certainly didn't have the fashion sense that they did.

Nervously, I opened the door.

Three stunned faces stared at me.

"It's good, right?" I smiled.

"Good?" Apple's mouth dropped open. "No, it's great!"

"I think so too." My smile spread even wider.

"It's your color and your style." Candy nodded. "I think it's perfect."

"Well, it doesn't matter what either of you think." Maby crossed her arms as she walked in a slow circle around me. "All that matters is what I think. I'm the Fairy Godmother, after all." She stopped in front of me and shrugged. "I mean, it is absolutely fantastic, but it's still my choice." She laughed. "Wrap it up!"

"Really?" I grinned.

"Really." Maby nodded. "You look gorgeous." She pulled out her phone and snapped a picture as I started to turn away.

"What's that for?" I glanced back at her.

"We need shoes and accessories to match the dress." She smiled. "You didn't think you were done, did you?"

I held back a groan. Maby's generosity was heartwarming, but I wasn't sure I could survive shoe shopping.

After another few hours of trudging through stores and then getting pedicures, we finally piled into the cab to head back to Oak Brook Academy. Though I was thoroughly exhausted, I was also thrilled to know that I had such good friends. Still, in the back of my mind, I heard a faint warning.

Don't get too comfortable, Sophie. Don't really believe this is your life.

We arrived at the school just in time for dinner. Though most of the store owners had plied us with coffee and snacks, I was still starving.

"I'll take the bags up to our room and meet you in the cafeteria." Maby slung the bags over her arms like a professional, then headed up the stairs to our room.

"Maby!" I called out to her as she reached the top step.

"Yes?"

"Thank you. Thank you so much." I smiled up at her.

"You're welcome, Fi. I had the best day." She smiled at me, then continued down the hall.

When I reached our table, I found that Mick and Wes were already there.

"Wow, she survived!" Mick laughed as he looked over at Wes. "You owe me twenty dollars."

"I guess I do." Wes rolled his eyes as he pulled his wallet out of his pocket.

"Excuse me?" I sat down across from them.

"Wes bet me that you wouldn't make it through half the day with those three." Mick rubbed his fingers together. "And now he's paying up."

"You bet against me?" I glared playfully at Wes.

"I just didn't think it would be the kind of thing that you would enjoy." He shrugged as he handed Mick his twenty dollars.

"I enjoy having such good friends." I tipped my head back and forth. "The shopping part, not as much."

"What about the pedicure?" Wes nudged my foot under the table with his foot. "Did you get sparkly polish?"

"Stop making fun of me!" I laughed.

"He can't help it." Mick grinned. "Ladies, did you accomplish your goal?" He looked up at Maby, Apple, and Candy as they joined us at the table. "Did you turn our little ragamuffin into a real girl?"

"Ragamuffin?" I stuck my tongue out at him. "I'm surprised you even know that word."

"There she is." Wes offered a slow-clap. "That's the real Fi coming out."

"Ouch, Fi, really." Mick clutched his chest.

"Stop!" Maby laughed. "You can answer that question for me." She pulled out her phone. "I just texted you both a picture."

"A what?" I looked over at her as my heart pounded.

"Relax, Fi, we're all friends here." Maby smiled at me.

"Maby, seriously?" I narrowed my eyes.

"Wow. Wait a minute, are you sure this is the same girl?" Mick looked at his phone, then looked up at me.

My cheeks burned. I looked over at Wes. He stared at his phone, then shrugged and tucked it back into his pocket.

"It's a nice dress."

The coolness of his voice struck me hard. *Yes, Fi, he's just a friend. It doesn't matter to him what you're dressed in, you're still just a friend.* I forced myself to look away.

"No, seriously, if I didn't have a date for the dance, I'd be asking you, Fi." Mick looked across the table at me. "That dress looks amazing on you."

"Like I'd say yes." I rolled my eyes and smiled at him. "I'm not going to have a date."

"Oh, yes, you are." Candy smiled. "I've already got three guys lined up."

"Lined up?" I stared at her.

"She needs to eat." Maby pushed my food toward me. "You're going to need your strength for the interviews."

"The interviews?" I stumbled over my words, then looked over at Wes.

If he cared that I was being set up he didn't show it.

TWENTY-FOUR

"The first interviews start tomorrow at lunch." Maby gave my knee a light swat. "So, be sure to be ready to make small talk."

"I'm not sure what that is." I winced.

"It'll be fine. We'll be right there with you." Apple looked over at Candy. "Right?"

"Right." Candy nodded. "Between the three of us, I'm sure we can pick someone who's just right."

"What makes you think that anyone would even want to go with me?" I raised an eyebrow.

"I would," Mick mumbled.

Wes took a bite of his hamburger.

"Are you kidding? You're new, you're cute, and you're one of us." Candy tossed her hair back over her shoulders. "You have plenty of attention."

As the other girls laughed, I squirmed in my chair. I wasn't sure that I wanted all of that attention. In fact, the only attention that I wanted was from someone who seemed far more interested in his dinner than he ever would be in me.

By the next morning I was a bundle of nerves, not just because I wasn't sure what would happen at lunch, but because

I still hadn't heard from my mother. It wasn't like her to go silent for this long. I wasn't sure what to expect, but I was convinced it would be something very bad.

I decided that if I hadn't heard from her by the end of the day, I would call Dale again and demand to know where she was. He'd said that he would have her call me, but how did I know if that meant he was actually going to be speaking to her? Maybe he was playing some kind of game to try to keep me away from her. The thought made me clench my teeth.

I wouldn't let anyone—not even a billionaire—treat my mother badly.

After a long shower to try to wake myself up, I grabbed a banana and headed off to class. I didn't want to chat with Maby, I just wanted some time to think.

I arrived to class a little early and settled at my desk. I flipped my notebook open and began to write. As the words poured onto the page, I felt some relief from the tension that had built up in my body. I wrote about my restlessness, about trying to fit into a place that I would never belong to, and about longing for something that I could never have.

By the time I looked up, many students had arrived.

Wes walked in, nodded to me, then settled in his chair. He didn't say a word. He didn't look at me longer than a few seconds. He did, however, watch another girl walk straight toward him. He didn't miss a second of her approach.

"Wes, is it true that you don't have a date for the dance?" She perched on the edge of his desk, her voice as smooth and sweet as the flounce of her hair and the curve of her hips.

"It's true." He shrugged as he looked up at her. "Why?"

"I thought you might want to know that I don't have a date either." She smiled. "At least, not yet."

"Not yet, huh?" He leaned his head back and smiled. "Do you have someone in mind?"

"Absolutely." She raised her eyebrows.

I looked away as my hands clenched into fists under my desk. It wasn't as if I didn't know he would date, that he would have his choice of girls to go to the dance with, but did I have to sit right beside him and witness it?

"Alana, back in your own seat, please." Mrs. Davis sighed as she walked into the classroom. "Let's go, people, we have a lot to cover today."

Alana walked back up front to her desk. Wes slumped down further in his.

I looked down at my notebook and tried not to breathe too loud. If there was ever a time I wanted to disappear, it was right then. The memories that had made me so happy not long before now haunted me. If I hadn't been alone with him, if I hadn't gotten so close to kissing him, would I even care that Alana would likely be his date?

Maybe it wouldn't be so bad if I did meet a few other boys. Why not? It might take my mind off Wes and even my mother— at least for a little while. The only problem was, I had no idea what I would say to them and I doubted that we would have anything in common.

But there was only one way to find out.

On my way to lunch, Apple caught me in the hallway.

"Not just yet." She smiled, then tugged me into the girls' bathroom.

"What's wrong?" I frowned.

"I just want to get you ready." She pulled out a tube of lipstick and a hair tie.

"Wait a minute, nobody said I'd have to do this." I backed away from her as she uncapped the lipstick.

"Oh stop, you can handle it. I'm sure you've been through worse." She approached me with a determined look in her eyes. "It's just to give you a confidence boost. Whenever I have to meet someone new, I like to look my best. It makes me feel more secure." She shrugged.

"I'm not sure that lipstick makes me look any better." I ducked my head out of the way as she attempted to swipe my lips with the tube.

"Oh sure, it's just a multi-billion-dollar industry for no reason." She rolled her eyes, then sighed. "Listen, just try it. Put some on, let me put your hair up, and then look in the mirror. If you don't like it, you can wash it off and take your hair down. Okay?"

"Okay. I guess." I closed my eyes as she glided the lipstick across my lips. I followed her instructions as she touched it up with a tissue.

When I opened my eyes again, she spun me around so that she could get to my hair. In just a few whips of her hand, she had it piled up in a messy bun that sent strands of it in all directions.

"Done." She clapped her hands. "Now, take a look."

I turned toward the mirror without much expectation of any change. But the Sophie that looked back at me was different. A splash of color on my lips seemed to even out my skin tone. The hair piled around my head framed it just enough to balance out the shape of my face. In less than five minutes, Apple had managed to change the way I looked.

"Wow, it's not too bad." I reached up and touched my hair.

"Don't mess with it too much, I didn't have enough bobby pins with me." She smacked my hand playfully. "So, are you going to leave it in?"

"Yes, I think I will." I took a deep breath and smiled at my reflection. It was another new thing to try.

I didn't want to disappoint her, but as we walked into the cafeteria together, I didn't feel any more confident about meeting my potential dates. The entire thing felt strange.

Seconds after I settled at the table, Wes joined us. He stared at me as he sat down at the table.

"Look at you." He smiled, then pulled out his phone. He began playing some kind of game.

His head was still down when a stranger with slicked-back hair and ice-blue eyes sat down across from me.

"Hi, I'm Ben." He met my eyes. "I'm here for the interview."

TWENTY-FIVE

I looked across the table at Ben and tried to remember how to speak. How could this boy be interested in me?

"Fi? You okay?" Apple nudged me hard in the arm.

"Yes, sorry." I forced a smile. "I'm Sophie." I offered him my hand.

"Pleasure to meet you, Sophie." He pulled my hand to his lips and placed a light kiss on the back of it. "If you choose me, I promise you'll have a night you'll never forget." He looked into my eyes as he released my hand.

"Okay." I cleared my throat. "What do you mean by that?"

"I mean—you can ask anyone—I know how to show a girl a good time." He sat back in his chair and smiled. "I'll buy you flowers, I'll wear you out on the dance floor, and I'll make sure you enjoy your walk home." He winked at me.

Somehow I thought the walk was going to entail a lot more than hand holding.

"And why do you want to go to the dance with me?" I narrowed my eyes.

"I think we could be good together." He took my hand again. "Just give me a chance and you won't regret it."

"Oh, is that what Monica thinks?" Wes took a loud slurp of his drink, then looked over at Ben.

"Why are you bringing her up?" Ben shot a look over at Wes. "You didn't have a problem picking up the pieces, did you?"

"Not cool, Ben." Wes glared at him.

"Don't listen to him." Ben looked back at me. "You and I would have a fantastic time. Think about it." He gave my hand a squeeze, then stood up and left the table.

"Well, that was weird." I frowned as I glanced over at Apple and Candy. "I'm not sure this was such a good idea."

"Relax." Candy waved her hand. "There are more to come."

"Sorry about that." Apple winced. "I thought he would be more charming."

"It's alright." I sank down in my chair and wished that lunch would be over.

A quick look over at Wes revealed that he had his attention on his phone again. I opened my mouth to say something to him, but before I could, another boy sat down across from me.

"Hi, I'm Nathan." He brushed his blond hair away from his eyes and smiled at me. "It's so nice to meet you, Sophie. I've heard a lot about you."

"You have?" My eyes widened as I didn't recognize him from any of my classes.

"Sure, I heard that you don't mind bending the rules a bit. You brought a boy into the girls' dormitory. You were out after curfew in the small library with someone. You hung out in New York City alone with a guy." He flashed me a smile. "I like a girl that's not afraid to push boundaries." He leaned close to me, his light brown eyes full of heat. "If you choose me, we could push lots of boundaries together. We don't even have to go to the dance. My dad has a private jet. I'll take you away from here—

anywhere you want to go. We could spend the night in Vegas together."

"Wow." I stared at him as I tried to process everything he was saying. "You want to date me because you think I have a bad reputation?" I shot a brief look at Wes. He was the one I was with on all of those occasions. Did he feel badly about the rumors that were apparently spreading across campus?

Wes continued to stare at his phone.

"Is it bad?" He shrugged. "There's nothing wrong with wanting to have a little fun. If that's what you want, I'm your guy." He stood up, then abruptly leaned across the table. His hand was in my messy bun before I understood what he was doing. His lips headed straight for mine.

"Hey!" I drew back in the same moment that Nathan was pulled back away from me.

"Nope." Wes glared at him as he pushed him from the table. "Not a chance, Nathan, not even the slightest."

"Shouldn't she be the one to decide that?" Nathan frowned as he looked back at me.

"He's right." I crossed my arms. "Whatever you and your friends think about me, you're wrong. So pass that along, got it?"

"Whatever." Nathan straightened his collar, then walked off.

"Scraping the bottom of the barrel or what?" Wes scowled at Maby. "You couldn't do better than him?"

His words stung. Of course they had to scrape the bottom of the barrel. It was ridiculous of me to think otherwise.

"I didn't know he was going to act like that." Maby sighed. "He talked a good game in his pre-interview."

"I think I've had enough." I stared down at my lunch as my cheeks burned.

"Don't give up yet." Candy smiled as she leaned close to me. "I have the perfect guy for you, trust me."

"No more." I sighed and looked up as Wes dropped back down into his chair. He must have been watching to see what Nathan did, but now his eyes were already back on his phone.

"Excuse me, am I interrupting?" A boy paused beside our table. His curly dark hair was cut close to his ears and his boyish features made him look a year or two younger than he probably was.

"Not at all, you're right on time." Candy led him to the chair across from me. "Punctual, I love that." She met my eyes as the boy sat down. "This is Bryce." She draped her arms over his shoulders and leaned her cheek against his. "Isn't he just adorable?"

"It's nice to meet you, Bryce." I shifted in my chair. After the first two candidates, I wasn't too eager to go through a third interview.

"You too." He looked into my eyes and smiled. When he did, his dark brown eyes seemed warm—warm and kind—as if he would never dream of doing anything to hurt me.

"Uh—some things you might want to know about me." He cleared his throat. "I've got pretty good grades. I really enjoy anything related to science. I play the cello." He looked up at Candy nervously, then back at me. "I've honestly never been to a dance before. So, I'm not sure what I should say."

I smiled at the way his hands fluttered, then clasped together. He seemed as uncomfortable as I was, but he was still there.

"I know this is really awkward and silly. You don't have to stay if you don't want to." I felt my face go warm as I looked away from him. How had I let myself be talked into something like this?

"Oh, I want to stay." He lowered his voice. "I begged Candy to let me have a chance."

"You did?" I laughed. "Why?"

"Why?" He shrugged. "I'd like to get to know you better. I've seen you around school and we're in a few classes together. I loved what you had to say about the lifespan of the fruit fly. I tried to catch you after class, but you never seem to have time to talk. You're always in a rush to get somewhere. So I thought this might be the perfect way for us to finally have a conversation. No pressure, though." He held up his hands. "I don't expect you to want to go to the dance with me when you don't even know who I am. But if you're interested, maybe we could spend a little time together over the next few days."

"That sounds good to me, actually." I smiled.

TWENTY-SIX

Throughout the week, I walked the halls with Bryce. I shared lunch in the courtyard with him. I found out that he loved to play chess, had two annoying little brothers, and hoped to one day be a scientist. Everything about him seemed sweet. I wanted more than anything to be excited by the sight of him. But each time I was with him, my thoughts shifted back to Wes—to that day on the carousel, to the way he'd been avoiding even looking at me since Monday.

By Wednesday, I'd accepted Bryce's invitation to the dance. Why not? He was kind to me and no one—more specifically, Wes—had asked me to go. If I was going to have to go to the dance, I wanted it to be with someone I could at least have a good time with.

On Thursday at lunch, I found myself staring at Wes again as he played with his phone. I was tempted to ask him if he had found a date to the dance yet, but I decided against it. It didn't seem as if he even wanted to speak to me anymore.

"Hi, Sophie." Bryce smiled as he walked up to me.

"Bryce, hi." I looked at him as he lingered beside the table. "Would you like to join us?"

"Sure, thanks." He set his tray down on the table next to mine.

Wes pulled his tray back some. Then he looked across the table at me.

From the look in his eye, I could tell that he wasn't pleased. It was the first time he'd look at me all day.

"Bryce, did you get your suit yet?" Maby pulled out her phone. "I sent you some options hours ago and you haven't answered."

"Sorry about that. I was in speech class and then music. Can't do a lot of texting there." He began to flip through his phone. "What do you think, Sophie?" He showed me the screen. "Would this one work with your dress?"

"I'm out." Wes stood up and snatched his tray off the table.

I watched as he walked over to return it and then stalked out of the cafeteria.

"What's with him?" I glanced at Maby.

"Wes is a little protective over our table." Apple scrunched up her nose. "He expects to be able to approve anyone who's invited to sit."

"Does that mean that I was approved?" I laughed.

"Never mind that." Maby pointed to Bryce's screen. "Are you going to pick one?"

"You should wear what you like, Bryce." I met his eyes. "Do you have a color you like? Or a certain style?"

"I don't really care." He shrugged. "You tell me what to get and I'll get it."

"Okay." I offered a faint smile. I found that Bryce didn't really have too many opinions about much. He mostly agreed with everything I said and never dug any deeper.

He's nice, though, I reminded myself—and he's not Wes— which was the most important thing.

With the craziness of getting a dress, a date, and getting to know Bryce, I'd been pretty distracted. I'd almost stopped worrying about my mother.

But as I settled into bed that night, my phone buzzed with a text.

I'LL BE SEEING you soon, honey. I'll explain everything then. Can't wait for our visit!

I STARED AT THE SCREEN. She was coming to visit me?

I dialed her number. It went straight to voicemail.

"Mom, you just texted me. Answer the phone!" I snapped at her on her voicemail.

Frustration boiled through me. What did she mean by a visit? Was she coming tomorrow? Over the weekend?

I couldn't fall asleep as I imagined the reasons for the visit. If she had to see me face-to-face to tell me what was going on, then it had to be really bad.

I woke the next morning after only a few hours of sleep. Immediately, the weight of my mother's impending visit threatened to make it impossible for me to get out of bed. But it was also the day of the dance.

Who was I? The Sophie that cleaned up her mother's messes? Or the Sophie that had a date with a boy who actually liked her, to a dance where she would spend the night with her amazing new friends?

"I want to be new Sophie." I pushed myself up off the bed. Whatever my mother was up to, I would find out soon enough, but I wouldn't let it stop me from enjoying the dance.

The day went by in a blur. Nervous couldn't begin to describe how I felt.

Dinner was served an hour early to give students time to

prepare for the dance. I couldn't help but notice that Wes wasn't there. I pushed the thought from my mind. No, I wasn't going to let Wes or my mother ruin this night for me. I would find a way to have fun, no matter what.

Back in our room after dinner, Maby took her time making sure every aspect of my make-up and hair was just right.

"Thanks for doing this, Maby." I met her eyes as she wound my hair around a curling iron.

"You don't have to thank me." She looked back at me. "We're friends, Fi."

"Still, thanks." I felt a rush of gratitude as I thought about how kind she'd been to me since I'd arrived at Oak Brook.

"There. Perfect." Maby smiled as she released my hair from the curling iron. "Plenty of bounce."

I looked at the curl in the mirror that she held up for me.

"How long will it stay that way?" I lightly touched the coil.

"It should last at least the length of the dance. Don't worry, we'll make sure we use lots of hairspray."

A hard knock on the door made me jump. "Who could that be?"

"Candy maybe. She said she might stop by to see how the curls turn out." Maby turned to set the curling iron down.

I walked to the door and opened it, ready to greet Candy with a smile. Instead, I found Wes, his eyes narrowed and his jaw tense.

"Wes, you shouldn't be here. We're going to get in trouble." I stared at him.

"I shouldn't be here or you don't want me here?" He raised an eyebrow as he stepped closer to me.

"It's fine, let him in." Maby waved her hand.

I wanted to say that of course I wanted him there. Instead, a muffled grunt escaped my lips as I stepped aside from the door to let him in.

"It's been some kind of show this week." Wes crossed his arms as he stood between the two of us.

"Show?" Maby looked at him. "What do you mean?"

"Parading Fi around like she's something to win at an auction, are you kidding me?" He shook his head. "What were you thinking?"

"We were just having a little fun, Wes." Maby laughed.

"And you." He looked directly at me. "How could you let them do that to you?"

"Don't act like I don't know what you're up to!" Maby stood up and glared at him. "I know exactly what you're playing at."

"What are you talking about?" He scowled at her.

"I know about the poem, Wes." She crossed her arms.

I took a sharp breath as Wes spun to face me.

TWENTY-SEVEN

"You showed her the poem?" His voice was edged with anger, though he didn't raise it. "I guess you two had a good laugh about me."

"I didn't, Wes, I swear." I looked over at Maby. "Why would you tell him that?"

"I'm telling him that because he needs to back off." Maby grabbed Wes's shoulder and turned him back to face her. "Fi is free to date whoever she wants and you are not going to stand in the way. Got it?"

"I can't believe this." He shook his head as he backed up toward the door. "You know what, you're absolutely right. She's free to date whoever she wants." He met my eyes. "I hope you have a nice time at the dance, but I won't be there. I'm not going to be part of any of this." He looked back at Maby. "She's her own person. If you were really her friend, you would know that. She doesn't have to do what you say, just because you think you're in charge of everyone." He pulled open the door, stepped out, then slammed it closed behind him.

"Wow." Maby shook her head. "Sometimes I just can't understand him at all."

I bit into my bottom lip. I didn't want to say anything, but I understood him just fine. He was right. Maby, Apple, and Candy had turned my dating life into their own little game. The truth was, I didn't want to go to the dance with Bryce. I didn't want to go to the dance with anyone but Wes. But that wasn't possible; he'd made that clear. I could have refused to go too. I could have told Maby the truth—that I didn't want to go—but she had done so much for me. I didn't want to disappoint her.

"I'm sure he has a lot going on right now." I forced a shrug.

"Maybe he does, but that's no excuse for acting like this. Never mind, forget about him, Fi. You are going to have a magical night, no matter what." She gave one of my curls a light tug. "Let's get you dressed."

As I let Maby do a final touch-up to my make-up, I tried to remain calm. But I couldn't help wondering what Wes would do instead of going to the dance. Would he find someone who wanted to stop thinking for a little while?

Tension flooded my muscles at the thought. I closed my eyes and attempted to fight off the rush of jealousy.

"No! No!" Maby sighed. "The mascara isn't dry yet!"

"Sorry." I frowned as I opened my eyes again.

"Hey, are you okay?" She looked into my eyes.

"Just nervous." I bit into my bottom lip.

"Not the lipstick!" She huffed, then pulled out the tube again.

By the time we walked out the door, I felt as if I couldn't touch my face, my hair, or the exquisite dress that I wore. Most of the girls were gathered in the common room where the boys were permitted to escort us to the multipurpose hall where the dance was to be held. I spotted Bryce as he walked toward me and smiled.

"Wow, you look amazing." He grinned at me as he slid a corsage onto my wrist.

"So do you." I looked over his well-tailored suit and smiled. "Thanks for inviting me, Bryce."

"Thanks for choosing me." He offered me his arm.

As he led me to the hall, I couldn't stop my heart from pounding—only it wasn't out of excitement. Despite Bryce's chattering in my ear, all I could think about was Wes.

Why had he been so upset? I hated the thought that he might really believe I'd given Maby his poem to read. He needed someone to trust and now he thought he couldn't trust me.

"Sophie, do you want a drink?" Bryce tugged slightly on my arm.

"Hm?" I glanced at him.

"Do you want some punch?" He smiled.

"Sure, thanks." I watched as he walked over to the punch bowl.

Enjoy him, Sophie. He's sweet, he's kind, and he's here.

Why couldn't I feel anything when he walked back toward me and handed me the cup? Why did I have to force my smile?

Despite the fact that I didn't dance well, Bryce was patient as he guided me through several dances.

"It's really just about the music." He stared into my eyes. "Just let it flow through you."

Music. Like the music of the carousel—the music that still played in the back of my mind as it had been ever since that night with Wes.

"Ouch!" Bryce drew his foot out from under mine.

"I'm sorry." I gasped as I stepped back.

"It's alright." He frowned, then shook his head. "Well, it is, but maybe we should just call it a night."

"The dance isn't over yet." I followed him off the dance floor. "Are you okay?"

"Sure, I'm fine." He turned to face me. "But I invited you to

159

the dance with me and I don't think you've been here all night." He shrugged. "If there's somewhere else you'd rather be, then maybe you should just go."

"Oh, Bryce." I sighed. "I'm sorry. You're right, I have been distracted. I just have a lot on my mind."

"I've heard the rumors about you and Wes." He frowned. "I had hoped maybe you would have better taste than that. But if that's the kind of guy you want, then enjoy him." He turned and walked away.

I was tempted to go after him, to make it clear to him that Wes and I weren't together and that we never had been. But what would be the point? He was right. I was distracted and I would continue to be until I straightened things out with Wes and figured out what was going on with my mother.

The music that pounded through the speakers, the laughter and the chatter of everyone around me—it was all suddenly way too loud. I pushed my way through the crowd to the door and stepped outside. A deep breath of the cool night air soothed me some, but not enough. Why did I have to make things so difficult?

Wes was a player and he didn't mine showing that off. So why did I want to be with him?

Maybe I was more like my mother than I realized.

As I walked back toward the dorm, I tried not to think about Wes. I tried not to think about where he was or who he might be with.

"Leaving early?" He stepped out from behind a statue in the courtyard.

"Wes." I bit into my lip as the sound of his voice stirred the memory of him whispering in my ear. "What are you doing here?"

"Waiting for you." He leaned back against the statue.

"Now you're the one spying?" I raised an eyebrow.

"I wanted to apologize." He looked down at the ground, then back at me. "For barging in earlier."

"Wes, I didn't show Maby the poem. She went into my room and found it." I moved closer to him. "You have to believe me."

"I do." He smiled and brushed his hair away from his eyes. "I don't know why, but I do. So what did she say to you when she found it?"

"I told her that it was just an assignment, that it didn't mean anything." I tried to meet his eyes, but he looked away before I could.

"Is that what you think?"

"Isn't it the truth?" My heart skipped a beat.

"Where's Bryce?" He glanced toward the door of the dance hall.

"I wasn't a good date." I pursed my lips as he avoided my question. "I knew I wouldn't be. You were right earlier." I looked down at my dress. "None of this is me. You can dress me up, but it won't change who I really am."

He stepped closer—a lot closer—to me. "You're beautiful, Fi."

"Sure I am, Maby put a lot of work into all this." I looked up at him and found his eyes waiting for mine.

"I thought you said you were a good listener?" He smiled as he wrapped one of my curls around his fingers. "I said you're beautiful." He shifted just a little closer.

Not again. My heart raced. What did it mean when he tipped his chin toward me like that? It seemed as if he could just tilt his head a little more and we would be locked in the kiss I longed for.

TWENTY-EIGHT

His breath coasted along the curve of my cheek and tickled across my lips.

I ignored Maby's warning and bit down on the lipstick that she'd so carefully applied.

"What were you really doing out here, Wes? Waiting for me? Or someone else?" I tipped my head back as I looked into his eyes.

"Ah, so I trust you..." He ran his thumb along the rise of my cheek beneath my eye. "But you don't trust me?"

I noticed the mascara smudged on his thumb as he pulled it away.

"It's not that." My chest ached with dread—and hope—as I looked at him. I wanted to ask him—once and for all—if he was trying to be a good friend or if he wanted something more. But I knew, as my heart raced, that I didn't want to hear the answer. I didn't want him to speak those words.

Sorry, Fi, but I don't think of you like that. Just the thought of hearing them made my legs weaken. How had I gotten so lost in him? How had I forgotten that the entire reason I was at Oak Brook was to create a good future for myself?

"Wes, my whole life has been complicated. From the day I was born, I was a mistake. I thought—I thought that maybe things were changing. Maybe things would be different here. But it's just as complicated. I still feel like a mistake."

"You could never be a mistake." His fingers curved around the slope of my waist.

I stepped back away from his touch. "Please don't." I struggled to hold back the tears in my eyes. "I know you're just being kind. But I can't handle it tonight." I turned and hurried back toward the dorm.

I carefully hung up the dress that Maby had bought for me. I set the shoes and accessories right beside it. Then I stepped into the shower and began to scrub every last bit of make-up off my face and hairspray out of my hair. Water rushed over my skin and mixed with the tears that slipped from my eyes.

I felt as if I'd made a fool of myself, not just with Bryce, but with Wes, because yet again I let myself believe that he'd been about to kiss me.

I spent the rest of the weekend in my room, despite Maby's knocking and pleading. I watched my phone for a text from my mother—a text that didn't come. I ate the food that Maby left outside my door, after she was sound asleep. I watched my phone for some sign from Wes that I wasn't an idiot to think he might like me.

Nothing.

Monday morning I had no choice but to emerge. I wasn't about to miss out on any classes, but I dreaded the thought of seeing Bryce in the hall or Wes in class. I'd tried not being invisible and it hadn't worked out well.

"You're alive." Maby crossed her arms as she watched me walk into the kitchen. "I was worried about you."

"I didn't mean to make you worry." I picked up an apple and picked at the skin. "I just needed some time."

"Was the date that bad?" Maby frowned as she studied me.

"It wasn't Bryce's fault. It was mine." I rolled the apple between my palms. "I never should have agreed to go with him."

"Fi, is this about Wes?" Maby stepped in front of me as I started toward the door.

"Of course not." I looked past her at the door.

"Are you sure? Because I haven't heard a word from him all weekend either." She lowered her voice. "You can tell me the truth."

"There's nothing to tell. I have to get to class." I stepped around her and through the door.

"Fi, wait!"

I just kept walking. I didn't want to think about Wes. Not at all. I didn't want to think about how he made me feel and how I had no control over it. Before I'd come to Oak Brook, I'd never experienced that before—a total loss of control.

As soon as I stepped into the classroom, I sat down and focused on my tablet.

I heard Wes come in. I heard him sit down at the desk beside mine.

"Fi." He whispered my name as the class began.

I ignored him and continued to stare at my tablet. I was aware of a knock on the door, but I didn't look up. I heard soft voices, but I didn't try to hear what they were saying.

"Sophie." Mrs. Davis's voice drew me out of my dazed state.

I glanced up from my tablet. Had I tuned out so much that I'd missed something? My stomach twisted. I could tell from the look on her face that something wasn't right.

"Yes?"

"Can you come up here please?" Her forehead pinched as she looked at me.

I stood up from my desk and started toward the end of the row.

Wes caught my hand and gave it a light squeeze.

I glanced back at him just long enough to see the concern in his eyes. When I turned back to the front of the classroom, a sing-song voice drifted in from the hallway.

"So-phie ba-by!"

Shock jolted through me. That was my mother's voice. A hint of relief took the edge off of my sudden annoyance.

She was alive. She wasn't in jail. Those were two good things. The chattering and laughter that followed her words, however, were not good things.

I hurried to the door and out into the hallway.

"Mom?" I stared at her as she spread her arms wide to greet me.

I took a step back. "Where have you been?"

"Oh, you know." She waved her hands and smiled. "Around!"

"You didn't return my calls or texts." I sighed. "Mom, I thought something terrible happened."

"Nothing terrible, no, freedom can never be terrible." She caught my shoulders and looked into my eyes. "Things didn't work out with Dale."

"What? Already?" I felt my heart drop. "What did you do?"

"Look, honey, things change. I can't help it." She shrugged. "One minute he's everything I've ever dreamed of, the next..." She sighed and lowered her voice. "Well, he's just very boring."

"Boring?" I stared into her eyes. "He's boring?"

"Yes. He's so proper and he never wants to have any fun. I mean, who wants to live like that?" She rolled her eyes.

"Mom, maybe you can work it out. Dale seems like a good guy." My heart began to race. If things were over with Dale, that meant I was about to lose everything.

"It's over, Sophie. Alright? He caught me with the stable

166

boy." She laughed. "How ridiculous is that? Like I always say, love is love, you can't fight it."

"Okay." I trembled as I took a breath. "So, we need a place to live. I'll get my things."

"No, wait." She smiled at me. "Dale insisted that you finish the semester. It's paid for. By then I'll be on my feet and have a place for you to come home to. Isn't that wonderful?"

"Wonderful?" I stared at her. "What about any of this is wonderful? Mom, when are you going to get it? It's not love you're feeling, it's fear! You go from one guy to the next because it's your way to escape from anything real!"

"Sophie." My mom's eyes were wide.

I glanced over my shoulder to see Mrs. Davis at the door. Wes was two steps behind her.

Mortified, I realized they'd heard everything.

I turned back to my mother, my eyes full of tears. "Please, just go, Mom. Please!"

"Fine." She shrugged, then winked at Wes. "I know when I'm not wanted." She turned and flounced off in the direction of the door.

It didn't seem to matter to her that she had just destroyed the fantasy I'd built around myself.

"Fi." Wes stepped out into the hall.

"I'll give you two a minute." Mrs. Davis pulled the door closed.

"Don't, Wes." I wiped at my eyes. "I don't want you to see me like this."

"It's okay." He wrapped his arm around my shoulders.

"No, it's not!" I pulled away from him and glared. The mixture of disappointment, hurt, and anger that raged through me spilled out all at once. "None of this is okay."

"We'll figure something out." He reached for me again.

"No!" I took another step back. "I knew this would happen.

None of this is real, it never has been. I never should have let myself believe it. Now I have to go back to the real world!"

"No." He wrapped his arm around my shoulder and this time didn't let me resist. He pulled me tight against his chest. "You're not alone in this anymore."

TWENTY-NINE

As good as it felt to have Wes's arms wrapped around me, I pushed my hands against his chest until he released me. As I took a step back, I looked into his wide eyes.

"I know that you're trying to comfort me, but this isn't going to do it." I took a slow breath, then another step back. "Right now, I just can't be around anyone."

I turned and continued down the hall of the school.

No, classes weren't over, but they were over for me. There was no point in attending if I wouldn't be a student much longer.

I walked through the courtyard—bombarded with memories of moments with Wes—and continued into the girls' dormitory.

My mother.

I pursed my lips as I pushed through the door. She was quite a piece of work. I knew the marriage wouldn't last, but it hadn't even been a month. Not even a month. My eyes burned again, but I refused to let more tears well up.

I had this coming, I knew that, and yet I'd let myself get lulled into the false sense of security that came with living in the little bubble that was Oak Brook.

I stepped into my dorm room and closed the door behind me. Maby would be at classes for the rest of the day. I'd made it clear to Wes that I didn't want to speak to him. Maybe it was unfair of me to do that, but it didn't matter to me anymore.

I'd been hoping that he would reach for me again, that he would want to put his arms around me, but when it finally happened, it was all wrong. He wasn't doing it because he was interested in me, he was doing it because he felt sorry for me.

Maybe he wanted to protect me from the world I'd come from. But it wouldn't be that bad going back to it. I knew what to expect, anyway.

I sprawled out on my bed and closed my eyes. We'd find some kind of cheap apartment to live in, the kind that came with pets already scurrying across the floor and a landlord that would threaten to evict at the first request for any repairs.

I'd end up in a nearby high school, the kind with metal detectors and armed guards. Maybe I would be safer there. I laughed into my pillow at the thought.

As my laughter faded, the tears began to flow. As angry as I was at my mother, I still regretted speaking to her the way that I had. I knew she couldn't be anyone different than who she was. I knew that I, as sad as it was, was the only person she had in the world. What right did I have to judge her? I'd nearly thrown away a great opportunity just because a pretty boy had distracted me.

We weren't as different as I liked to think.

At some point, I drifted off to sleep.

I woke up to music playing in the living room.

Maby was home.

Faint light drifted through the curtains in my bedroom. It was evening, probably a short time before dinner. My stomach clenched at the thought of eating anything. All I wanted to do was stay in bed and drift away on the sound of the music that played.

A soft scraping sound against my carpet made me lift my head off the pillow. I saw a piece of paper glide across the floor. I thought about ignoring it. What could it say that I wanted to hear? But Maby had been such a good friend to me, I knew it wasn't right to ignore her.

I forced myself out of bed and picked up the note.

I HAVE CHOCOLATE. Lots of chocolate.

I LAUGHED as I wiped at my cheeks, still sticky from tears. Chocolate did sound very, very good. I took a shaky breath as I opened the door to the living room.

"Hey, hon." Maby opened her arms to me. "I heard you had a rough day."

"Yes." I murmured as I let her wrap her arms around me.

She hugged me close and sighed. "My mother always says that I didn't come with an instruction manual. So she just had to wing it."

"That's an interesting way to put it." I smiled as I pulled away from her. "It seems like you two are close."

"Yes, I'd say we are." She shrugged. "We don't get to spend as much time together as we used to—now that she's so involved in her political career—but she is always there for me when I need her. I'm sorry you don't have that, Sophie." She tucked my hair behind my ear. "But you have it from me."

"That's sweet, Maby. I'll believe you when you show me the chocolate." I grinned.

"Oh, she can joke, that's a good sign!" She laughed and led me over to the sofa. Assorted candies were spread out across the coffee table. "I picked us out some nice music and I thought we could have a little chat."

"I'm not sure I'm up for talking." I picked up one of the candies, then plopped down on the sofa. "But these might help."

"It's alright if you don't want to talk. I understand. It's probably all still very raw." She picked up a candy as well and popped it into her mouth.

I relaxed against the sofa as the chocolate melted in my mouth. I wanted the sweet taste to soak right into my veins. Anything to make the ugly dread that had become an elephant on my chest go away.

"Actually, I'm the one that needs to talk." She turned to face me, crossing her legs underneath her. "Are you up for listening?"

"Sure." I met her eyes, eager to be the kind of friend to her that she'd been to me, even if it would only last a little while longer.

"So, I might have been a little hasty about some things." She folded her hands in her lap. "You see, in case you haven't noticed, I can be a little—well..."

"Bossy? Controlling?" I grinned at her.

"Or maybe—protective?" She raised an eyebrow.

"Yes, protective." I laughed and picked up another piece of chocolate.

"Alright, fine, controlling." She rolled her eyes. "But that's only because I usually know what's best." She bit into her bottom lip. "Usually."

"Maby, what's this about?" I studied her. Was she upset that she would have to get another roommate?

"When I found that poem that Wes wrote—I'll be honest, I was shocked." She frowned.

"No, not Wes, please." I closed my eyes. "I will talk about anything but Wes."

"I'm sorry, but that's what I need to talk about." She took my hand. "Fi, I think I've made a terrible mistake."

"What do you mean?" The seriousness of her tone made me look straight at her.

"I told you to be careful around him, I told you that he doesn't stick with one girl, but I didn't tell you that he's never written a poem for a girl before." She sighed. "Even when he was with Candy, he didn't do things like that. And yes, things were rough between the two of them, but he was honest with her from the beginning about it not being anything serious. She just didn't want to hear it."

"What are you trying to say?" I shook my head. "The poem didn't mean anything."

"That's what I'm trying to say." She squeezed my hand. "I think it means everything. I think he meant every word of it and I can't let you leave here without telling you what I've been feeling."

Stunned, I shrunk back against the sofa. "You told me not to fall for it."

"I meant it. I thought I was protecting you. But after he showed up here, the way he talked about you, the look in his eyes... Fi, I think he really has feelings for you."

THIRTY

"Are you serious?" I stared into Maby's eyes.

"I am." She frowned. "I wish I had realized it sooner. I feel like I wasn't a very good friend to you or to Wes, because I kept trying to push you two apart. But I only did it because I didn't want either of you to get hurt. Now that I see how much you really care about each other—well, I just thought you should know."

"I'm not sure what to say." I picked up another piece of chocolate as my mind spun between panic and elation.

Was she right?

Maby knew Wes better than anyone else. If she thought he had feelings for me, if she thought that he meant what he'd written in the poem, then maybe it was true.

I remembered what he'd said to me in the hallway earlier that day. He said I would never have to be alone again. But I thought he meant as a friend.

There was one thing I knew now. I couldn't continue much longer without knowing for sure.

"Maybe I should go talk to him."

"I think you should." Maby picked up her phone. "He told

me was hanging out in the courtyard a little while ago. He might still be there."

"Are you sure about this?" I frowned, even as my heartbeat quickened.

"I've known Wes for a long time. I've never seen him heartbroken over anyone. When he told me what happened to you today, I could have sworn he was ready to burst into tears."

"Wes?" My eyes widened.

"Right?" She shook her head. "It shocked me too."

"If he's that upset then I definitely should talk to him." I looked toward the door.

My original plan had been to stay holed up inside as long as possible. But if Wes was out there, hurting, I owed it to him at least to get everything straight between us.

I thought about the times I'd wondered if he wanted to kiss me. What if he had? What if each time I pulled away, he felt as torn up inside as I had when I walked away?

The thought drove me out of the dorm and into the courtyard.

Maybe he wouldn't be there. Maybe he'd already gone back to his room. Maybe he wasn't upset about me leaving but upset about something else.

With my heart in my throat I walked toward the fountain in the center of the courtyard. I could see him there, his head tilted down as he looked at his phone, his hair hanging forward hiding his eyes.

A shiver crept along my spine. How could he be so gorgeous? It shouldn't be physically possible.

"Wes?" I murmured his name as I paused beside him.

"Fi!" He jumped to his feet and dropped his phone in the process. "Sorry, let me get that. Just a second." He grabbed his phone, then straightened up and pushed his hair out of his eyes. "Are you okay?"

"I guess." I shoved my hands in my pockets and shrugged.

"I was going to text this to you, but now I can show it to you myself." He held his phone out to me. "I told you we'd figure something out."

"What is this?" I took the phone from him and began to read over information about a scholarship.

"With your grades, I'm sure you'll qualify. Mrs. Davis already said she'd write you a letter of recommendation." He smiled. "So maybe you'll be able to stay."

"You talked to Mrs. Davis about me?" My heart pounded a little faster.

"Yes, she was concerned." He pointed to the phone. "Isn't it great? I can get you the paperwork so you can apply for it."

"Wes, this is sweet, but I don't think it's going to work. These kinds of things take a long time to process and usually they have to be done for the beginning of the year." I frowned. "I'll look into it, though."

"That's all I'm asking." He reached for his phone and his fingers collided with mine.

I felt a shower of sparks shimmer through me as I looked up at him. In that moment, I knew I had to know. I didn't want to go one more day without finding out the truth.

"You told me that I could trust you, right?"

"Of course." He shifted closer to me. "I know that I haven't always given you good reason to—I mean, with the way I've acted. But I've told you things I've never told anyone else."

"Have you told me everything that you wanted to tell me?" I searched his eyes. "Is there anything that you might be holding back?"

"I'm not sure what you mean." He looked over at the fountain, then the ground. His cheeks reddened.

"Wes." I narrowed my eyes, determined to get a straight answer. "The poem you wrote about me?"

"Yeah?" He glanced back at me. "Is Maby telling you things about me again?" He frowned. "I can't say that she's wrong, but Fi, you know that's not me, not who I really am. Don't you?"

"Maby did tell me some things about you, yes." My muscles tensed as I wondered if I could go through with finally asking him. "She told me that you might have meant everything that you wrote in that poem—that you might have meant it to mean something and not just be part of an assignment."

"Oh." He licked his lips as he took a slight step away from me. "And what did you say?"

"I said that it was just an assignment. That you couldn't feel that way about me." I grabbed his hand as he started to step back again. "Don't, Wes. Not this time. I want the truth."

"You mean you really had no idea?" He curled his fingers around mine and pulled me close to him. "You didn't know that when we were at the carousel, I tried to kiss you? You didn't know that night after the dance?"

"I didn't," I whispered. He'd pulled me so close to him that it seemed as if the rest of the world had disappeared. "Why didn't you just tell me?"

"I did." He touched my cheek with his free hand and looked into my eyes. "I wrote you a poem."

"Wes." I took a sharp breath as he continued to stare at me. "You're serious?"

"I didn't think you wanted anything to do with me." He gave a short laugh. "Every time I got near you, you would find a way to get away. Not this time, though." He leaned forward as he guided my head toward him.

For an instant I was caught up in his scent, in the warmth of his skin and the way his fingertips felt stroking my hair. Finally we would kiss. Finally when it was far too late.

"Wes, no." I pulled away from him at the last second before I would finally feel his lips on mine.

"Fi!" He groaned and slid his arms around my waist. "Why?"

"Because it's too late." I couldn't believe my own words as I spoke them, but I couldn't stop them either. "Nothing can happen between us now. My life is a mess. What I need right now is a friend, someone that I can trust."

"Then that's what you'll have." He let his arms fall back to his sides. "Whatever you need, that's what I'll be."

THIRTY-ONE

"Thank you, Wes." My heart ached as I looked at him.

This whole time, if I had just been brave enough to tell him the truth, or tip my lips toward his, things could have been very different. But as I walked away from him, I knew that it really was for the best.

What if I had kissed him? What if he had told me the truth from that first moment when my body buzzed with anticipation? Then where would I be?

Heartbroken and forced to leave the first real relationship that I'd ever have. There couldn't be anything good about that.

When it came down to it, it was best for me not to have anything to do with Wes. And not just Wes, but Maby and the others as well. By the end of the semester, I would just be a memory to them and they would move on with their lives. I would move on with mine too. It wasn't about things being fair or unfair, it was just how it had always been.

Later that night, as I was about to crawl into bed, my phone rang. I thought it might be Wes, but instead it was my mother.

"Hi." I sprawled out across my bed.

"Hi," she whispered. "Are you still mad?"

"No, Mom, I'm not mad." I closed my eyes. "You have to do what you think is right."

"I begged him to take me back, Soph, I really did. But he wouldn't forgive me." Her voice trembled. "I'm sorry, I really messed things up for you this time."

"It's alright, Mom." *It wasn't alright, but what could she do about it now?*

"No, it's not." She sighed into the phone. "I thought when I married Dale that I would make everything better for you. I thought that I would finally be the kind of mother that you deserve. I don't know why I do the things I do. I'm so sorry."

"It's alright, Mom." I willed myself not to cry. "I don't belong here anyway. We both knew that."

"Don't say that. Don't ever say that. You're not any less than the rest of those kids there. You are so, so smart. I've always told you how smart you are, haven't I?"

"Yes." I smiled some. "Remember that time you carried my solar system project five miles because the bus driver wouldn't let us take it on the bus?"

"Yes. It took us a long time, but we got there."

"Yeah, we did. And I got an A." I laughed. "Even though I was very late for school."

"I wish I'd done better for you, hon."

"Like you said, Mom, it might take us a long time, but we're still going to get there."

"You're so good, Sophie. You're so good to me. I love you so much."

"I love you too, Mom." I took a deep breath. "Do you have somewhere to stay?"

"Yes, don't worry about me. I'll let you know when I find us a place. I'll try to make it nice. Then guess what? We get to decorate!" She laughed.

"Yup. I'm really tired. I'm going to sleep now."

"Goodnight, Soph."

"Night, Mom." I hung up the phone.

Even though she hadn't brought good news, I was relieved to know where she was and what had happened. At least now I knew what to expect.

The next morning I thought about not going to class. What was the point? But I couldn't risk being kicked out before the semester was over. Who knew where or with whom my mother was staying? I didn't want to be stranded in New York City. Instead, I forced myself to go through the motions of my usual morning.

While Maby ranted to me about a girl in one of her classes, I nibbled at toast and pretended to listen. I hoped that she would get a good new roommate.

I walked to class, still in a fog as I tried to process all the changes in my life.

Wes had feelings for me. That still shocked me every time I thought about it.

I drifted off into a fantasy of the two of us back on the carousel, of me leaning down to meet his lips, of our first kiss being shared in that perfect moment.

"Sophie?" Mrs. Davis's voice snapped me to attention.

"Yes?" I looked at my teacher, standing just outside the classroom door.

"I'm so sorry about everything that happened yesterday." She frowned.

"Thanks. I'm sorry if I disrupted the class." I looked down at my feet.

"It's okay." She took a slow breath. "I wish I didn't have to tell you this, but I looked into the scholarship that Wes wants you to apply for. I'm afraid it requires you to have been a student at this school for at least a year."

"Oh." I nodded as my heart sank. I hadn't really thought it

would work out, but my last glimmer of hope faded with her words. "That's alright. Wes told me you wrote me a letter; thank you."

"I was happy to do it. Sophie, I know you haven't been here long, but you are a very talented writer. No matter what happens, I hope that you will continue on with your education." She tipped her head toward the door. "Come in, I'm going to enjoy you while I have you."

"Okay." I managed a small smile. I'd had a few teachers compliment me over the years and it always meant a lot to me, but to have a teacher at a school as prestigious as Oak Brook pay me a compliment? It gave me a burst of confidence.

Not long after I sat down at my desk, Wes arrived and sat down at his.

"Hey, Fi." He looked straight at me.

"Morning." I flashed him a brief smile.

"Can we talk?" He reached for my hand.

"I don't think that's a good idea." I pulled my hand away. Then Mrs. Davis started the class.

When it was over, I was the first one out the door. I continued that trend for the rest of the day. If I saw any of my friends in the hall, I made an effort to go in the opposite direction. It was better to prepare myself now for the inevitable. The more time I spent with them, the harder it would be for me to say goodbye.

At lunch, I hid out in the library. At dinner, I holed up in my room. When Maby knocked to say good night, I pretended to be asleep. I heard her whisper outside my door.

"Fi, I'm here if you want to talk."

I remained quiet. There was no reason to answer her. I wasn't Fi anymore. I was Sophie again. And Sophie didn't have any friends.

And that's how it would be when I started at my next

school. I would be targeted for showing up in the middle of the year out of the blue. I would be bullied for the mere fact that I was new. I would hide. I would ignore them all. Soon they would forget about me.

I just hoped that I still knew how to disappear.

THIRTY-TWO

By Thursday, I had turned dodging my friends into an art. Wes wasn't texting me anymore. Maby had stopped knocking on my bedroom door. If I saw Apple or Candy in the hallway, I found a room to duck into. Mick, on the other hand, continued to wave and shout at me. I just smiled at him and continued by. It wasn't easy.

Friday afternoon I spotted the five of them gathered in a knot near the door that led to the courtyard. It hurt to see them all gathered together. I wanted to be in the middle of whatever conversation they were having. As usual, Maby seemed to be giving instructions to everyone else. But Wes stood right beside her. When he spoke, I wished I could hear what he said—or just hear his voice at all.

"Don't do this to yourself, Fi." I forced myself to turn away. As I walked down the hall toward the girls' dormitory, I heard footsteps run up behind me.

"Fi, slow down for a minute." Wes caught me by the shoulder.

"I have to go." I wriggled out of his grasp.

"No, you don't." He stepped in front of me. "Is this really

how you're going to play things now? You're going to act like I'm a perfect stranger?"

"I'm not playing anything. I just need some space." I adjusted my backpack on my shoulder. The feel of the smooth material reminded me that Maby had given it to me. I planned to give it back to her. If I kept it, I'd just have to sell it or someone would try to steal it. There wasn't much point to that.

"No." He moved in front of me as I tried to step to the side.

"What do you mean, no?" I stared at him. "I thought you said that you would give me whatever I needed?"

"I did and I meant it." He shifted in the other direction as I again tried to step around him.

"This is a funny way of showing it." I frowned.

"I don't think that being alone and shutting out all of your friends—all the people that care about you—is what you need." He narrowed his eyes. "You may think so, but that doesn't make you right."

"You think you know what I need?" My lips were tight as I shook my head. "You don't."

"I think I do, yes." He continued to block me from walking past him.

"Stop it, Wes!" I placed one hand against his chest to give him a firm push. But the moment I felt the warmth of his skin through his shirt, all of the strength went out of my arm. "Please."

"I'm worried about you, Fi." He placed his hand over mine and held it against his chest. "We all are." He tilted his head toward the others, who'd gathered around me.

"I'm fine." I pulled my hand away as my cheeks grew hot. "I'm doing what I need to do—to make this easier—okay?"

"It's not okay, no." Wes shook his head. "Just because you might have to leave at the end of the semester, that doesn't make us any less your friends."

"That's nice of you to say." I took a step back and found Maby right behind me.

"It's not something that we're just saying." She crossed her arms as she met my eyes. "It's the truth. Pushing us away isn't going to change anything. So this afternoon, you belong to us."

"Maby, I can't do this." I began to panic as I started to tear up. I didn't want them to see how upset I was.

"You know me better than that, hon." She draped her arm around my shoulder. "What I say goes. Let's go." She steered me toward the door.

"Where are we going?" I sighed. I could have fought back. I could have walked away. But the truth was, I loved having them around me again and it meant a lot to me that they still considered me a friend.

"To our place." Wes walked on the other side of me.

"We planned a surprise picnic!" Apple clapped her hands together and grinned.

"Apple!" Candy rolled her eyes. "It's not a surprise if you tell her."

"Oh, right." Apple frowned. "Sorry."

"I got real fried chicken from the city." Mick grinned as he met my eyes. "They never feed us that here—something about carbs and grease. Whatever! I'm a growing boy!" He smacked his muscular stomach.

"Sounds delicious." A smile came to my lips, one I couldn't resist.

"There she is." Wes nudged me with his elbow. "Fi's back."

"Temporarily." I grinned.

I followed them to the storage building—to the fort that they kept a secret just for them and that, thanks to Maby, I'd been welcomed into. It smelled like fried chicken, mashed potatoes, and cherry soda. But it wasn't the smell that made everything so delicious. It was the company.

For a little while I forgot about the difficulty that I faced. I remembered what it was like to be surrounded by people who wanted to be around me. They'd gone to so much trouble to give me a special afternoon, to brighten my spirits.

But as the sun began to set, I felt the pressure of the next day coming. And the day after that. And the eventual day when I would have to say goodbye to all of them. The others began to head off to the dorms, but Wes and Maby lingered behind.

"I'll clean up." Wes began to gather up the paper plates and cups.

Maby sat down beside me. "Thanks for letting us do this." She took my hand in hers. "We've all been worried."

"I didn't mean to worry you." I sighed. "It's just that I've never had to do this before. I've left a lot of schools—I've moved more times than I can count—but I never really had anyone to say goodbye to. I'm not handling that part well."

"Because you're trying to handle it by yourself." She hugged me. "We're not going to forget about you, Fi, no matter what you think."

"Thanks, Maby." I hugged her in return. "I guess we should get back."

"Wes might need some help with that trash." Maby winked as she hurried out the door.

I stood up to help him, but Wes wasn't cleaning anymore. He had my notebook in his hands.

"Wes, what are you doing?" I grabbed for it. "You're not reading that, are you?"

"I can't stop reading them." He looked up at me. "Fi, you should turn one of these in with the application for the scholarship."

"Wes, stop." I took the notebook from him and closed it. "I can't even apply for the scholarship. It's only for people who have been here for a year."

"I'm sure they can make an exception." He frowned.

"Just let it go, Wes." I shook my head. "It's not going to happen. There's nothing that anyone can do. Filling my head with hope and possibilities—that only makes it harder." I walked toward the door.

"You're not the only one, you know." He caught me around the waist and guided me back toward him. "You're not the only one that this is hard on."

"I'm sorry." I felt his lips graze my cheek and my heart threatened to burst. I wanted nothing more than to turn into his arms and give in to my desire to finally kiss him.

But that would make it so much harder to say goodbye.

THIRTY-THREE

The memory of his lips was burned into my cheek as I walked back to my dorm room. My skin tingled where he'd touched it. That couldn't be normal, could it?

I stepped through the door to my room and found Maby on the sofa. My heart raced as I considered telling her about what had happened.

But I couldn't. If I shared it, it would be real. The fact that I walked away from him would be real.

"Back so soon?" She raised an eyebrow. "I thought you might spend a little time with Wes."

"No." I dropped down onto the sofa beside her. "That's exactly what I don't need to do."

"Why?" Maby looked over at me. "Wasn't I right about the poem?"

"Yes, you were. But that doesn't change anything." I sighed. "You know, it's like this strange form of torture. I'm getting everything I want, only to watch it all be taken away. I never imagined that Wes could be interested in someone like me or that I would be interested in someone like him, for that matter. Then all of a sudden—bam, it happens. I never thought I'd have a circle of friends that I could trust that cared about me and yet here you all are." I leaned forward on my knees and closed my eyes. "I just wish it could have happened at a different time. The truth is, when I'm gone, life will go on. We'll e-mail or text or maybe even tag each other in some posts, but eventually that will fade. While you all have stories to share, I'll be somewhere completely different, outside of everything."

"It doesn't have to be like that." Maby grabbed my hand and squeezed it. "I talked to my mother while you were gone. I told her about your situation. She agreed to pay for your tuition for the rest of the year. But the administration won't let us do it without your mother's permission—or yours, for that matter." She smiled. "That will give you time to get things with the scholarship figured out. If not that, then something else. It means that you get to stay here with us." She smiled as she looked into my eyes. "All you have to do is say yes."

"Maby." I sank back against the sofa. "I can't thank you enough for the offer, but it's too much. There's no way I can accept that from you and your mother. Besides, it would just be delaying the inevitable."

"Why are you fighting this?" She stood up and groaned. "Why can't you just say yes?"

"Because it's not just about me." I looked up at her as my chest tightened. "My mother—I don't think she can take care of herself on her own. She won't pay the bills on time, she'll hook up with some guy that drinks too much or has his hands in the wrong kinds of businesses. It was one thing for me to be here when I knew that she was with Dale. I knew that he would take care of her, that she would be fine with him. But now?" I shook my head. "I'm sorry. I know she doesn't seem like much to you, but she's still my mother. I can't leave her alone out there."

"I'm sure you love your mother very much." Maby crouched down in front of me and took my hands. "But Fi, you are going to be eighteen next year. You're going to be an adult, legally able to make all of your own decisions—live where you choose, with whom you choose." She frowned as she searched my eyes. "How long are you going to keep taking care of her while you give up everything you deserve?"

"I don't know." I pursed my lips. "I hadn't really put a date on it."

"Maybe it's something you should think about." She sighed, then shook her head. "I can't make you say yes and take my offer. I can't make you stay here, even though I like to think that I have control over everything. But it's time you got your head on straight, Fi. I'm not going to sit here and just watch you wallow in your misery, while you still have a chance to enjoy what you have right now. I can't promise you that you won't have to leave or that things will magically get better. But I can promise you that if you don't enjoy what you can, you'll regret it."

She stood up and released my hands. "You made Wes fall in love with you. He has never—and I do mean never—cared about a girl the way he cares about you. Isn't that worth fighting for? Isn't our friendship worth enjoying for as long as you can?" She crossed her arms. "You may think that you are protecting yourself by isolating yourself, but you're not. It won't hurt any less when the day comes to say goodbye. The difference will be that you will have to face the fact that you wasted what time we all had left together." She turned and stalked off toward her room. "Wallow if you want, but I won't stand by and watch it anymore."

"Maby." I started to follow after her, but when she slammed her door shut, I stopped. She couldn't possibly understand. What was the point of trying to explain it to her?

Yes, I wished that things had happened differently with Wes. I wished that I knew what it was like to go on a real date with him, to hold his hand while we walked down the street and to feel absolutely alone with him in a little bubble of love. There were all kinds of things I wanted to experience with him. But I didn't have all kinds of time.

I had just enough time to get to know him, to find out that I was right about what an amazing person he was, only to then have to say goodbye.

I couldn't do it. No matter how Maby pressured me—no matter how much sense she made—she couldn't understand, because she had never been forced to walk away from anything. Her generous offer only reminded me that we would never be the same.

I closed myself off in my room and sat down on my bed.

I stretched out in my bed and looked up at the ceiling. Her words replayed through my mind even when I tried to shut them out.

You made Wes fall in love with you, isn't that worth fighting for?

Wes, in love with me?

I closed my eyes. No one had ever even asked me on a date.

What if I'd turned around and kissed him? What if I stopped caring about what was to come and just said yes? Could he possibly love me?

What if I left Oak Brook Academy for good without ever finding out if it might be true?

I fell asleep with these questions circling through my mind.

THIRTY-FOUR

I woke up in the middle of the night. I'd fallen asleep too early and my body was ready to get up. But my mind and my heart were not. My heart still ached from the night before and my head was on full alert. Warnings blasted through my thoughts.

Don't get used to this soft bed.

Don't even think about what Wes might be doing right now.

Don't look at that dress hanging in your closet.

Don't...just don't.

I squeezed my eyes shut. It would be easier if I could go back to sleep, but I couldn't. I'd slept hard and my body was done resting.

I sat up in my bed and tried to ignore the warnings that continued to blare through my mind. I grabbed my backpack and unzipped it. Then I turned on the light beside my bed.

Writing helped me figure things out. Maybe if I put some of these feelings down on paper, I could finally get control over them. If I didn't, I wasn't sure that I would ever be okay again.

"Was it worth it?" I wondered out loud as I tapped my pen against the paper. I'd gotten everything I wanted and now I had to give it up again. Would it have been better if I'd never had it in the first place? If I had never come to Oak Brook? If I had never met Maby and her friends? If I had never met Wes?

I began to write.

I wrote about the first time I met Maby. I wrote about the fort and our visit to the Statue of Liberty. I wrote about feeling like an outsider and then being drawn into an exclusive group of friends who saw something in me, something worthy of their attention and friendship.

As the words flowed, I already had my answer.

It had been worth it—and so much more. I wouldn't trade the times I'd had with my friends, even if it meant it could spare me the pain of losing them.

But what about Wes?

I wrote about the first time I saw him, how quickly I judged him, how sure I was that I would never want anything to do with him. I wrote about feeling his hand on mine for the first time and the way his eyes gleamed when they looked into mine. I wrote about discovering that I could feel more than I ever imagined I could, that I could be reduced to making silly choices, just because he looked in my direction.

"Wes." I whispered his name as I continued to write.

Then there was no stopping my imagination.

Was he lying awake in his room too? Was he feeling the same deep longing that I was for him?

I thought about the cruel way that I'd walked away from him and how it would feel if he had been the one to do it to me. He'd confided in me that he'd never felt a real connection with a girl before. Then he'd confessed that he felt it with me.

And what did I do?

Did I pull him into my arms and admit the same thing?

No, I told him it wasn't possible, that it couldn't happen. I told him all the things I'd been telling myself since the first day my heart had skipped a beat.

Maby had asked me if his love was worth fighting for and I didn't even answer her. I didn't even consider it. Because he couldn't possibly love me.

But what if he did?

My heart pounded harder. My pen fell to the floor.

All at once I understood what an idiot I'd been. I'd gotten so caught up in the idea that everything had to be perfect—that Wes and I had to have plenty of time to get to know each other —that I needed to belong to his portion of society in some way.

But the truth was, it didn't need to be perfect. It just needed to be him and me and the feelings that we shared.

I couldn't go back in time and never arrive at Oak Brook Academy. I couldn't refuse to have met him. I also couldn't go forward in time and find out how things would turn out.

All I could do was be in that exact moment, sitting in my room at a little past four, dreaming of what it would be like to kiss him.

Only it didn't have to be a dream. It didn't have to be something that I just imagined.

I was the only one stopping it. I was the only one declaring it impossible.

I picked up my pen and began to write again. As the words flowed out of me, I wasn't writing for myself. I was writing for the one person I hoped would still be willing to listen. I didn't want another day to pass without Wes knowing exactly how I felt and that I wouldn't trade a single minute with him, even if it meant enduring heartbreak later.

When I finished, I pulled the paper out of my notebook and read the words over to myself. It was everything I wished I'd said when he'd confessed his feelings for me. It was everything I hoped wasn't too late to share with him.

There was only one way to find out.

Convincing myself to take that next step—to be seen—took

several hours. It took changing my clothes multiple times, even though I didn't have that many outfits. It took looking in the mirror and putting my hair up and then pulling it down. It took putting on a bit of lipstick and then wiping it off. It took every heartbeat that slammed against my chest in defiance of the warnings that still blared through my mind.

Then finally, I opened my bedroom door. I walked past Maby, who offered me a sleepy good morning, and straight out through the door into the hall. I marched down the stairs that led to first floor and then continued out into the courtyard. It didn't matter what my hair looked like, what clothes I'd chosen, or whether or not I had lipstick on.

All that mattered was the paper I clutched in my hand and the words I'd written on it.

My knees wobbled as I climbed onto the edge of the fountain. My hands trembled as I clutched the paper tight.

I noticed the students that began to fill the courtyard, looking in my direction. I heard them whisper. But I didn't care. I just continued to wait for the right pair of eyes to find me.

"Fi, what are you doing up there?" Apple paused in front of me with a puzzled look. "Are you okay?"

"I will be." I didn't look at her, I just continued to search.

A small crowd of curious onlookers gathered around the fountain. It grew with every minute that passed. I saw texts being sent. I noticed some cell phones pointed in my direction. I had never been more seen in my life.

But it didn't matter.

There was only one person that I wanted to see me.

THIRTY-FIVE

My legs had begun to ache.

It occurred to me that he might not even show up. He might not decide to walk through the courtyard. He might decide to skip classes for the entire day.

But I resisted the urge to get down.

A few seconds later, I heard footsteps approaching. The crowd parted, as if they knew that he was the one I was waiting for.

He walked toward me, his hands buried deep in his pockets, his eyes on the ground in front of him.

"Wes." The moment I spoke his name, he looked up at me and smiled.

Then his smile faded as he assessed the situation.

"Fi, what are you doing up there?" He frowned as he held his hand out to me. "I'll help you down."

"Not yet." I met his eyes. "I have something that I want to say to you."

"Okay?" He glanced around at the others who had closed the circle around us. For the first time I noticed that Maby was there, her arms linked with both Candy and Apple.

"Go for it, Fi!" Mick shouted from the back of the crowd and pumped his fist in the air.

I smiled as I looked back at Wes. Yes, I was nervous. Yes, I knew that he might think I was ridiculous and might have already decided that I wasn't worth the trouble. But with the support of my friends, I felt a little more confident.

"Fi, whatever it is, just tell me." Wes stepped closer to me. "You can tell me anything."

I breathed in deeply and mustered all my courage. "Once I dreamed of something great, something more than I ever had. A warm home and a full plate, just one day without feeling sad. I dreamed of a brighter day, a time when I could be proud. A place where someone wouldn't always say, nope sorry, you can't pay, then you're not allowed. I dreamed of all these things that I'd never had before. I thought I dreamed it all, that I could never want for more." I dared to glance up from the paper and found that he stood right at my feet, his hands placed on the stone fountain on either side of them.

He looked up at me, his eyes wide as I continued.

"Never once did I dream of you, not even a glimmer of what you make me feel. Never once did I wish that it could be true, because I had no idea that a dream like you could even be real."

I licked my lips and took a short breath. "Wes, you're everything I never knew was a possibility. You've changed who I am just with that goofy know-it-all smile you wear and those eyes that see right into the depths of me. And no matter how hard I fight it, you've still shown me how much you care." I tucked the paper into my pocket and held my hand out to him. "I'm sorry it took me so long to admit it, but now that I can see, I hope that you'll share with me this very minute and everything that it might possibly be. I hope that you can still see me."

My fingers trembled as they stretched out to him. I could

feel my knees threatening to buckle from standing on the stone ledge for so long.

"I always will, Fi." He took my hand and with a soft tug, he pulled me down into his arms.

Around us a cheer erupted from the crowd. Mick's voice resonated over everyone's. Maby gave a squeal as she clapped. I'd never been so pleased to have an audience as Wes hugged me tighter.

Over the speakers, the bell for the first class chimed. The other students scattered in all different directions. Some of them had missed breakfast and others had to run to make it to their class on time. But they didn't seem to mind.

As Wes set me down on the ground, I looked into his eyes. I remembered how close we'd come to kissing so many times. And finally, I wasn't going to go another minute without knowing what it was like.

"You wrote that for me?" He smoothed my hair back over my shoulders. His warm touch brushed along the slope of my neck.

"I did." I searched his eyes. "I'm sorry for what I said, Wes. I don't care if we only have a few weeks or a few days, I want to spend that time with you."

"I do too." He smiled and touched my cheek. "This is all new to me too, Fi. I know how scary it is. But when I'm with you, I don't feel afraid at all."

Then kiss me, I wanted to shout at him. Instead, I decided I wouldn't wait any longer. I lifted up on my toes and reached for his lips with my own.

Just then, the second bell for class chimed.

I closed my eyes as my lips neared his.

"Oh no, we're late!" Wes took a step back, which made me stumble forward. "We have to go." He grabbed my hand.

"What?" I stared at him. "Since when do you care about getting to class on time?" I tried to pull him back toward me.

"I don't have time to explain." He looked back at me, straight into my eyes. "You just have to trust me, okay?"

I sighed. I didn't want to trust him, I wanted to kiss him. But the insistent look in his eyes made me nod.

He held my hand as we hurried to class together.

Yet again, the warnings in my mind blared. I couldn't seem to help myself.

You were too foolish, you drew too much attention. Now he's never going to want to kiss you. He's just using class as an excuse to get away from you. He's already lost interest. He's already moved on.

I remembered Alana, perched on his desk, quite eager to ask him to the dance.

How stupid had I been? Of course he had his choice of girls to spend time with. When I turned him down, he'd probably felt rejected, he'd probably needed to blow off some steam. I'd waited too long to tell him the truth, and now obviously, it was too late.

We reached the classroom just as Mrs. Davis was closing the door.

"It's about time." She frowned at both of us. "Get inside."

When we stepped inside the door, Wes let go of my hand.

It was in that moment that I became convinced that his mind was on other things. I walked to my desk and slumped down in it.

I heard a few whispers around me. Of course they would whisper about me after what they'd just seen. Of course they would think I had lost my mind. Maybe it actually was a good thing that I wouldn't be back for the next semester.

Mrs. Davis walked to the front of the class. "Quiet down, everyone, that's enough." She clapped her hands together.

I looked over at Wes, who stared down at his tablet. Was he playing that game again? Was that all that was on his mind?

I closed my eyes and wished that I could disappear once and for all.

It wouldn't be long before I wasn't even a memory at Oak Brook Academy.

THIRTY-SIX

"Now, there's an announcement I need to make." Mrs. Davis began to walk back and forth in the front of the classroom.

I watched her, but I wasn't terribly interested. I still felt as if I'd made a fool of myself. It was hard for me to concentrate on anything else. I did notice that Wes had set down his tablet.

I looked over at him, hoping that he would at least look at me or give me some sign of how he was feeling.

Instead, he stared straight ahead at Mrs. Davis.

In all the time that I'd known him, I was certain that was the first time I'd ever seen him pay attention in class. Why today of all days did he find Mrs. Davis so fascinating?

He just doesn't want to look at me.

I sighed and closed my eyes.

"Wes, would you come up here, please?" Mrs. Davis paused and looked straight at him.

My heartbeat quickened. Why was she calling on him? Was it because we had shown up late? Was she going to make an example of him? I winced as I realized that it would be all my fault.

"Sure." Wes stood up from his desk.

I tried to meet his eyes so that I could whisper an apology, but he refused to look at me. Instead, he walked up to the front of the classroom and stood beside Mrs. Davis.

"As many of you know, our newest student Sophie ran into some personal issues." She clasped her hands together in front of her. "Even though she's only been here for a short time, I've enjoyed having her in my class and I'm sure that many of you have enjoyed having her here as well."

A few of the other students looked in my direction. I squirmed in my chair and forced a smile. Was this some kind of going away party? Wasn't it a little early for that? I had no idea what to expect. But whatever it was, I could tell from that knowing smile on Wes's lips that he had something to do with it. Was that why he didn't want to look at me? Because he didn't want me to figure out the surprise?

Suddenly it dawned on me that this might have been why he'd been so eager to get me to class on time.

As I met his eyes, he spared me a quick wink.

"Sophie, would you come up here, please?" Mrs. Davis smiled at me.

I hesitated. The last thing I wanted to do was stand in the front of the classroom. Everyone had just watched me recite poetry to a boy that just about any girl in the school would have been eager to go on a date with. Did I need to further humiliate myself?

"Let's go, Fi." Wes held his hand out to me. "Trust me, remember?"

I couldn't help but smile.

I remembered.

I remembered that he had found a way to reach me when no one else had been able to. I remembered that he had pulled a far too eager boy away before he could cause me any harm. I remembered that he had confessed to me the reason why he had a reputation as a player—he'd wanted me to know who he really was. Most of all, I remembered that I'd promised myself that I would live in the moment. Not in the past and not in the future.

And in that moment, I wanted to feel his hand around mine, no matter the reason for it.

I walked up to the front of the class and took his hand.

As I turned to face the other students, I noticed that most smiled at me. Even though I hadn't had much of a chance to get to know them, they seemed to wish me well.

"Now, Sophie, when Wes came to me and asked me to write a letter of recommendation for you, I didn't hesitate. I know how bright you are and how dedicated to your studies you've shown yourself to be. Unfortunately, it turned out that the letter wouldn't help matters, since the program Wes wanted you to be a part of was only extended to students under certain parameters." She frowned. "I thought it would have to end there. But Wes..." She looked over at him and smiled. "Wes wouldn't take no for an answer. He did his research, contacted the people he needed to, and went as high up in the administration as he could to make sure that you had the opportunity you so richly deserve."

She walked over to her desk and picked up a piece of paper. When she walked back over to me, I held my breath as she continued.

"Because of all his hard work and relentless determination, he managed to turn that no into a solid yes." She held the paper out to me. "Sophie, I'm happy to officially extend to you a scholarship, not only for the remainder of this year, but for next year as well. Oak Brook Academy is happy to permanently welcome you as a part of our school." She smiled. "That is, if you're willing to accept?"

I stared at the paper that hung between us. A big part of me wanted to snatch it from her hands. But there was still a small voice inside me that reminded me that I had to make sure my mother was okay. She would be lost without me. But how could I turn down a chance to have everything I wanted? I looked past Mrs. Davis to Wes.

"You don't have to answer now. I'm sorry, I thought this would be a good way to surprise you." He wrapped his arm around me.

I thought about the last conversation I'd had with my mother. I remembered the tremble in her voice when she talked about what she wanted for me, what she felt I deserved, and how she wished she could do that one thing for me.

Would it really be helping her to turn down the very gift she'd attempted to give me? Did she really need me as much as I thought she did or was that just my way of keeping myself from moving forward into a brighter future?

"Yes." The word slipped from my mouth as I took the piece of paper from Mrs. Davis's hand. "Yes, thank you so much." I looked from her to Wes. "Wes, I can't believe you did all this for me."

"I'd do it again and anything else I could to give you what you need—what you deserve." He stared into my eyes. "Yes, Fi, I will always see you." He pulled me into his arms and in the same moment he tilted his chin, I lifted mine. Our lips collided, not in a light brush, but a passionate kiss that elicited cheers from the students around us.

"Okay, that's good. Yes, that's enough." Mrs. Davis pushed us apart as she laughed. "Now then, we do have actual work to get to." She shooed us back toward our desks.

As I turned to make my way to my desk, Wes caught my eye and grinned that goofy grin of his as he reached for my hand.

The kiss had been wonderful, but that moment when he caught my hand—just to remind me that he was there—that moment was everything I'd ever wanted.

EPILOGUE

I looked into the mirror at the reflection that stared back at me. The person in the mirror had mascara on one eye and not the other. Her lipstick was a little crooked. But that's not what I saw.

I saw a glow in my eyes that I'd never seen before.

I knew that Wes was waiting for me down in the courtyard, probably perched on the same fountain that I'd stood on a few weeks before when I'd declared my love for him.

It had been a whirlwind since then.

I'd made arrangements to accept the scholarship. My mother had found a new home with the stable boy and insisted that this time it was true love. I laughed as I recalled that conversation.

Maby knocked on my bathroom door. "Hurry up in there! You can't leave Wes alone in the courtyard for too long, you know he attracts those girls like flies."

I laughed as I popped the door open. "I'm almost done. Are you sure you don't want to come with us?"

"Are you kidding? You got a pass from Mrs. Reed to have a

solo celebration date with Wes. You can't possibly want a tag-along." She shook her head. "Besides, Alana is coming over to watch a movie."

"Oh yeah?" I raised an eyebrow as I applied mascara to my other eye. I still didn't have the hang of putting it on. But it didn't really matter. I was only using it because it was a special night. "Are you sure she's not flitting around Wes in the court-yard?" I thought about the way she'd tried to tempt Wes into asking her out to the dance weeks before.

"Leave the girl alone, Wes was free and single then, remem-ber?" Maby grinned. "You can't blame her for trying. But she's not like that at all. I've gotten to know her since we've been in debate club together. I think she's pretty sweet. I might even want to take her to the fort sometime."

"Oh wow." I stepped out of the bathroom and smiled. "Things are getting serious."

"Well, you know, I used to have this friend and we would hang out and do stuff together. And then this guy whisked her off her feet, so I've had some free time lately." She rolled her eyes and wiped a smudge of lipstick from my bottom lip.

"True." I smiled at her. "I'll see you later tonight." I gave her a quick hug, then walked out the door.

With each step that brought me closer to Wes, I felt more excited. I'd thought the initial buzz between us would fade pretty quickly. Instead, it seemed to grow each time we saw each other.

As I pushed through the door that led to the courtyard, I nearly stumbled over Mick.

"Sorry, Fi." He smiled as he took a step back.

"Hanging out by the girls' dormitory, are you, Mick?" I raised an eyebrow as I looked at him.

"Just out for a walk." He shrugged and stretched his arms above his head.

"Sure." I lowered my voice. "It wouldn't happen to have anything to do with the fact that Alana is coming over to hang out with Maby, would it?"

"Huh? Is she?" He coughed. "I don't know anything about that."

"Uh-huh." I nudged his shoulder. "Just don't let this little crush turn into full-blown stalking, okay?"

"You're crazy." He laughed and shook his head. "Nothing like that is happening." He pointed toward the fountain. "I saw Wes over there waiting for you."

"Thanks." I tipped my head in the other direction. "Oh, and here comes Alana."

"What?" He spun around so fast that his hair ruffled in the breeze.

"Gotcha." I laughed as I walked toward the fountain.

"Cute, Fi, real cute." Mick continued to linger by the door.

"Is he still over there waiting for Alana?" Wes stepped around the side of the fountain and held his hand out to me.

"Not at all, he's just out for a walk." I grinned, took his hand, and pulled him close. "Sorry if I kept you waiting."

"I'd wait as long as you need." He kissed my cheek. "Our reservations, though..."

"Reservations?" I cringed. "I told you nothing fancy."

"Well—I mean, there's fancy and then there's fancy. I only had to call a week ahead to get this reservation—not like I needed to book a month in advance or anything." He guided me toward the sidewalk. "Don't worry, you'll love it."

"I'm sure I will." I clenched my teeth. Paying more money for a plate of food than some people earned in a week wasn't my idea of fun, but I knew that Wes had different tastes than me.

"Have you heard from your mother?" He walked closer to me as we headed off the campus.

"Yes, she's all settled in. Blissfully happy—for the moment." I smiled.

"Maybe it'll last a little longer this time." He sighed.

"Maybe." I tightened my grasp on his hand. "You know, I used to think that she was crazy. Well, crazier than I think she is now. She used to tell me—'Once you feel it, Soph, you'll never want to stop.'"

"But she's right." He paused in the middle of the sidewalk and slid his arms around my waist. "I didn't know that until now either."

"She was right." I nodded as I looked into his eyes. "I guess at some point, she felt it and she's been trying to find it again ever since. Nothing's ever guaranteed in life, I get that. My whole life has been full of changes. But I couldn't be happier to be able to share this moment with you."

"I feel the same way." He leaned down in the same moment that I raised up on my toes and our lips locked together in a familiar, but still thrilling kiss.

My fingertips tingled and my toes wiggled inside my shoes. He stirred something in me that I hadn't even known existed. He pulled me just a little closer and the kiss lasted just a little longer.

As he took my hand again, my mind buzzed with all kinds of warnings.

Don't forget to enjoy this, Fi. Don't worry about the past or the future, just stay right here in this moment.

As he gazed into my eyes, with the sun setting just behind him, I couldn't quite take a breath.

I had no idea when I'd arrived at Oak Brook Academy that I'd discover what it was to be truly happy.

It wasn't the wealth, it wasn't the food, it wasn't the opportunities that the school afforded me. It was the friends I'd met and the choices I'd made that had led me here.

Nothing was perfect, but I didn't want it to be. I wanted it to be exactly as it was in this moment—with me and all my imperfections—holding hands with a boy who happened to think I was pretty great.

ALSO BY JILLIAN ADAMS

Amazon.com/author/jillianadams

OAK BROOK ACADEMY SERIES

The New Girl (Sophie and Wes)

Falling for Him (Alana and Mick)

No More Hiding (Apple and Ty)

Worth the Wait (Maby and Oliver)

A Fresh Start (Jennifer and Gabriel)

Made in the USA
Monee, IL
03 December 2021